The Champagne Killer

The Champagne Killer

HUGH PENTECOST

A Red Badge Novel of Suspense

DODD, MEAD & COMPANY · NEW YORK

ISBN: 0-396-06611-9
Library of Congress Catalog Card Number: 72-2342
Printed in the United States of America
by Vail-Ballou Press, Inc., Binghamton, N. Y.

The Champagne Killer

Chapter 1

THE CROWD INSIDE and outside Madison Square Garden in New York was bedlam loud, but not out of hand. Three quarters of them seemed to be teen-aged girls, shrieking and squealing in a kind of orgiastic frenzy.

Johnny Sands was coming back.

Of course there were preliminary excitements before Johnny Sands would put in an appearance. Some of the greatest names in show business edged their way through the narrow, roped-off alley the police had set up on the sidewalk and on through the lobby. As limousines pulled up at the curb disgorging beautiful women, furs, jewels, handsome sun-tanned men in tow, the crowd surged forward, pleading for autographs. There were top political figures, basking in the glamour atmosphere, pausing hopefully as cameras clicked. There were some of the richest men in America, anonymous, but exuding an aura of importance and power, accompanied by elegantly gowned women wearing the lacquered masks of total security.

Johnny Sands was coming back after two years in retirement; Johnny Sands with his trumpet and his haunting voice. He was coming back to head this benefit for the Foundation to Combat Respiratory Diseases. He was the honorary national chairman, and the rich and famous were thronging to Madison Square Garden, knowing they would be hooked for a million dollars before the night was over. They were ready and not reluctant. Johnny Sands would play and sing for his money.

Of course there would be others; famous actors would do a turn, there would be other singers, rock groups, jazz groups. It would be a great evening's entertainment. Murray Kling, top comedian and perhaps only second to Bob Hope as a master of ceremonies, would preside. But the star turn would be Johnny Sands. He was all that mattered really to the crowd inside and outside the Garden. The people on the street would wait for Johnny to arrive, and they would wait to hear him because loudspeakers had been set up on the streets for them. Members of Johnny's committee would pass through that outside crowd with baskets, collecting small change. Inside the checks would be astronomical.

The celebrities were still coming; celebrities and those who hoped to be mistaken for celebrities. There was a tall, thin man, apparently in his mid-thirties, wearing a maroon dinner jacket, with gold thread woven into the fabric. His cummerbund and tie matched the jacket. His hair was gold, worn longish but perfectly styled. His profile looked like a Greek god's, stamped on an old coin. He was accompanied by an exotic, dark girl, sultry, exciting. The tips of her fingers rested on the man's sleeve, not for support or protection. The gesture seemed to say "this man is mine." They had to be *someone!*

A young girl, flushed with excitement, ducked under the rope.

"Please, may I have your autograph?"

The golden man gave her a languid smile. "You don't want my autograph," he said. "You don't know who I am."

4

The girl's laugh was shrill. "Of course I know. Please!"

The man looked back. They were holding up the glamour parade. He took the notebook and pen from the girl and wrote one word on the blank page: QUIST. The girl looked at it and her face froze. She didn't have the faintest idea who he was after all.

Quist and his lady moved on into the lobby. A young man in a conventional dinner jacket was signaling to them from north side near the door to the Garden's private offices. The couple edged toward him. The young man was sweating.

"Hi, Lydia," he said to the girl. "Julian, there's hell to pay."

"Oh?" Quist said.

"He may not make it."

"Who may not make it?"

"Johnny. Sands."

Julian Quist's pale blue eyes narrowed. "You're kidding."

"No."

"That drunken bastard!" Quist said.

"No, no. It's not that, Julian. You'd better come into the office. We can't talk here."

The young man opened the door marked PRIVATE and Quist and his lady followed him in. There were half a dozen people in the room including Murray Kling, the prospective MC, and a devastated-looking woman whom Quist recognized as Mrs. Delbert Scheer, vice-chairman of Johnny Sands' committee, the person who really did the work.

"The problem is," Murray Kling said, "whether we try to hold them or tell them straight out that he may not show and watch them leave by the thousands."

"Oh God!" Mrs. Delbert Scheer said.

"Will somebody be good enough—" Quist began.

5

Everybody started to talk at once.

"Bobby!" Quist said, his voice sharp.

The young man who had met him in the lobby wiped his face with a white linen handkerchief. "Johnny's plane out of Chicago," he said. "Twenty minutes out they got word of a possible bomb planted on the plane; turned back. God knows what other flight he can get." A phone was ringing in the background.

Everybody was talking again. The Garden manager, who'd answered the phone, waved to Quist. "For you," he said. "I think it's Sands."

Quist elbowed his way to the phone.

"Julian?"

"Yes, Johnny." You couldn't mistake that voice.

"Isn't this hell?"

"Where are you?"

"Airport. Chicago. Leaving here in ten–twelve minutes."

"Which will get you here at midnight," Quist said. "Was there a bomb?"

"False alarm. Some sonofabitch playing games."

"You realize this place is jammed now?"

"Great!" Johnny Sands laughed. He sounded like an excited kid. "Tell 'em what's happened. It's in the news, on radio and TV. They'll know it's no gag. Tell 'em I'll sing for them till breakfast if they'll wait."

"It's a long time to wait, Johnny."

"They'll wait," Johnny Sands said. "Gotta go. Be seeing you, pal. Flight Seven-fourteen. Have me met."

Julian Quist Associates is one of the top public relations firms in the country. They handle the accounts of big businesses, politicians, actors, musicians, ballet companies, art galleries, museums. Julian Quist is the presiding genius. The luscious girl with him at the Garden that night was Lydia Morton. Looking like a glamorous high

6

fashion model, Lydia is actually a brilliant writer and researcher for Quist. She is also other things to Quist. The young man in the conventional dinner jacket was Bobby Hilliard, looking like a shy, young Jimmy Stewart, an "associate." Quist had handled special situations for Johnny Sands in the last few years and had done the buildup for this particular benefit at the Garden. Everyone in the Garden office seemed to be looking to him for answers.

"Johnny's leaving Chicago in five or ten minutes," he told the worried group. "Flying time is a little under two hours. The flight number is Seven-fourteen. Bobby, arrange for a police escort from the airport."

"Right."

"He can't make it till eleven-thirty at the earliest," Murray Kling said. "What are we supposed to do out there?"

"Start the evening as though nothing has happened," Quist said. "They won't expect him early in the program. I'll try to dig up a newsman they know—Walter Cronkite, someone like that. We'll put him on with the news story —and let him give them Johnny's message."

"What message?"

"He'll sing for them till breakfast if they'll wait."

"God sake, I've got a girl waiting for me for the weekend," Murray Kling said.

The corner of Quist's mouth moved faintly. His eyes were on Lydia Morton. "Me too," he said. "But this isn't for Johnny, Kling. It's for a hundred thousand sick people."

"What if I run out of jokes?"

"Do your strip-tease act," Quist said. "Better get it rolling."

When you talk about Johnny Sands you are talking about a giant in the entertainment world. He had been fifty-six years old when he retired two years ago. He had

7

been at the top of the heap then, a multimillionirie, a legend in his time. He belonged in the same bracket in the music world as Frank Sinatra and Bing Crosby. His career had followed a not unfamiliar path. He had started somewhere in the Midwest with a small band, playing the trumpet and doing the vocals. The band had come to New York, playing in one of the Fifty-second Street hot spots. Eventually they had been booked into the Paramount Theater. Rudy Vallee with his megaphone had begun there, Sinatra with the squealing girls in the balconies. Johnny was just one of a group, but featured. But when he stepped forward to indulge in his pyrotechnics on the trumpet the place went wild, and when he sang the girls screamed and moaned. Johnny Sands was in. His records broke records. *Variety*, the show-biz bible, called him a white Louis Armstrong. They were wrong. Johnny Sands was his own man. He was like no one. He could phrase a song like Sinatra, he could blow a horn like Armstrong, he could cause riots among the female population like no one else.

Johnny married four beautiful women in his time. He gambled, he dissipated, he was followed around by an army of yes-men. For all his flamboyance Johnny was a softhearted man, a kind man. He had done more benefits in his time—for no money—than anyone in show business. He had helped more down-and-outers and old-timers than could be counted. He was brash and loving, wild in his public behavior and disciplined in his work. There was no such thing as competition he feared, or jealousy for others in his field. He had helped dozens of young singers on the way to success. They said he owned half of Los Angeles and would give away a hotel for breakfast if someone wanted it badly enough. Johnny Sands was unique, an original, a figure in his time who would never be forgotten.

So Johnny Sands was late. It was ten-to-one the audience would wait for him.

Quist staged it shrewdly. Murray Kling started the show with his customary monologue, taking swipes at everyone from Nixon to Queen Elizabeth, from Martha Mitchell to Mohammed Ali. The audience was happy. Johnny Sands was coming back. A famous rock group shook the rafters. A young male singer who said he "owed everything to Johnny Sands" did his thing. A famous actor made a preliminary plea for the charity. A girl singer, paying tribute to Johnny, made the male members of the audience happy.

It was at that point that Quist slipped in his newsman. He hadn't been able to find a Walter Cronkite on such short notice, but Brian Marr would do.

"I want to read you a news bulletin," Marr told the audience, which had received him politely. "Flight Sixty-two out of Chicago, on its way to New York, was turned back about an hour ago because they were tipped off that a bomb had been planted on the plane. Among the passengers on that plane was Johnny Sands."

There was a gasp of horror from the audience, cries of "No, no!" Marr had to hold up his hands for silence.

"Johnny's all right!" Marr shouted into the microphone. "I promise you, Johnny's perfectly safe!"

There were sighs of relief, then applause. Then the audience waited for the big disappointment.

"Johnny left Chicago about forty minutes ago," Marr told them. "He should arrive in New York in about an hour—or a little more. A police escort is waiting to bring him to the Garden. And he sends you a message. 'Tell them I'll sing for them till breakfast if they'll wait for me!' "

Thunderous applause greeted this. Murray Kling took the ball again, sweating a little. He had probably an hour

9

and a half to go. He looked around the great arena. No one was leaving, but he sensed a slight change in his audience. They were challenging him now—challenging him to be good.

It was a long haul. The singers sang again. The rock group did their stuff with a little less vitality. A jazz combo that filled the gaps seemed frenzied. People wandered out to the refreshment stands and the rest rooms—waiting. And then, when it seemed it had been going on forever, in the middle of a long involved joke Murray Kling was trying to sell, there came a distant sound from the lobby—the high clear notes of a horn.

It was like magic. There was a swell of sounds from twenty thousand throats.

Johnny Sands was back. He came skipping down a distant aisle, golden horn raised to the sky.

> When the saints go marching in,
> When the saints go marching in—

The jazz combo picked it up. Down the aisle he skipped, up onto the platform. He made a sweeping gesture of invitation to the crowd to join him, a gesture with the horn. Then he was at the mike, singing.

> "When the saints go marching in,
> When the saints go marching in—"

Women screamed. Thousands of voices rose to join him. And finally it came to an end and he was holding out his arms for silence.

"You're all dolls!" he said.

A roar of delight. Sitting next to Quist in about the tenth row, Lydia pressed herself against her man.

"God, I never thought there was any sex in a horn," she said.

"Mistake," Quist said. "It's in the man. He doesn't look

a day over forty, and a well-cared-for forty at that."

Johnny was calling for silence again. "You've waited so long," he said. "Give me ten minutes to wash my face and get into my monkey suit, then I'll stay with you as long as you want. Forever, if you say so!"

He came down from the platform and up the aisle that would bring him past Quist and Lydia. He was followed by Eddie Wismer, his go-for, looking like Mickey Rooney. He stopped by Quist. Close-up Johnny looked strained and tense—looked his age.

"I got to talk to you, pal," he said to Quist.

"Sure, Johnny," Quist said. "Tomorrow. Come to my place about eleven tomorrow morning and we'll drink breakfast."

"Tonight, when this is over!" Johnny said. "I need your help, pal. Jesus, how I need your help!"

And he was gone, with young girls grabbing at his clothes.

Chapter 2

MUSICALLY, it was a night nobody was apt to forget. Johnny was at his best and, seemingly, inexhaustible. He sang and played Cole Porter and Jerome Kern, Gershwin and Berlin, the Beatles and Burt Bacharach. He called for requests from the audience and he denied no one. Don Edwards, who had been Johnny's accompanist for twenty-five years, seemed to be slowly wilting under the bright lights, but Johnny appeared to grow in strength and energy. Old timers remembered stories of the days back in the twenties when, after a performance of a musical comedy at the old Winter Garden theater, Al Jolson used to come down on the stage apron and ask, "Wanta hear more? I feel like singing," and go on into the early hours of the morning.

Brian Marr, the newsman, had been intrigued enough to stay on after his announcement to see what happened. There wasn't a vacant seat in the house, but he sat on the steps in the aisle next to Julian Quist. In the few minutes while the crowd waited for Johnny to wash his face and change into his bright gold dinner jacket, Marr said:

"It must have been quite a night at the Chicago airport. The bomb scare, and then while they were searching the plane for the nonexistent bomb, some Joe was murdered in the men's room—shot to death."

"Anyone we know?" Quist asked, in his dry voice.

Marr shrugged. "Nothing on it yet."

Later, when Johnny was going full blast, Marr shook his head in disbelief. "I swear he's better now than he ever was."

"Two years' rest," Quist said. "His pipes were worn pretty raw when he quit."

"Drank a lot, didn't he?"

"And still does," Quist said.

"I don't understand why he quit," Marr said.

"Had all the money he could ever spend; had all the adulation he could ever use."

"Never," Marr said. "He eats it up. Watch him. He loves this crowd, loves them for loving him. He'd rather sing than drink! Why did he quit?"

"Maybe a whim," Quist said. "Maybe tonight will bring him back."

Eddie Wismer, the little Mickey Rooney guy, came up the aisle and stopped by Quist.

"Johnny says to forget about tonight," he said. "He'll see you for breakfast."

"Eleven o'clock," Quist said.

"Check," Eddie said.

"He sounds fine, Eddie," Quist said.

"The greatest! Always was and always will be," Eddie said.

Quist lives in a duplex apartment on Beekman Place. There is a wide terrace overlooking the East River, not far from the oblong box that is the United Nations Building. Very few people have ever penetrated to the second floor of that apartment. It consists of Quist's bedroom, which also faces the river. It's a large, airy room painted in pale pastels. It might have seemed bare to most people, because there were no decorations on the walls, no paintings, only dark blue curtains that could be drawn across the windows to shut out the light. There were only two pieces of furniture in the room; a huge, king-sized box-spring bed, and a bedside table on which rested a telephone, a small intercom box that connected with the first floor, and an electric clock.

The bedroom opens into a bathroom, large, containing a glassed-in shower, a sunken tub, in pink marble, as large as a small swimming pool, a washbasin and medicine cabinet. You can walk out of the bathroom into Quist's dressing room. This room is, if anything, larger than the bedroom. There is a bureau, modern in style, endless built-in drawers, a full-length, three-sided tailor's mirror, and acres of closets which are said to contain over a hundred and fifty suits, or combinations of slacks and coats, evening wear, and God knows what else.

Down the hall is another small, conventional bathroom which opens into another room. This contains a dressing table with theater lights flanking the mirror. There is a chaise longue but no bed. In the closets are women's clothes. Who they belong to is nobody's business.

On the morning after Johnny Sands' remarkable performance at Madison Square Garden, Quist suddenly became aware, through his subconscious perhaps, that something was happening. The phone on the bedside table didn't ring, but a little red light blinked on and off. This was the phone from the building's lobby. He turned, carefully so as not to disturb the girl who slept beside him, and glanced at the electric clock. Six A.M.! Early, but very early, morning sunlight was sifting through the windows.

Quist picked up the phone. "So what the hell?" he said softly.

"I'm sorry, Mr. Quist," the attendant in the lobby said.

14

"I know what time it is. But there is a Mr. Sands here who says it's an emergency."

"Drunk?"

"No, sir."

"Put him on."

Johnny's voice, high and brittle, said: "Life and death, like they say in the melodramas, pal."

"If it isn't you'll go out by way of the terrace—nineteen floors to the street," Quist said.

"I gag you not, pal," Johnny said.

"Give me five minutes," Quist said.

"I'll wait outside your door," Johnny said. "Open up when you're ready."

Quist put down the phone and turned to the sleeping girl. Her dark hair was spread out on the pillow. She looked, he thought, like an innocent child. He leaned over and kissed her gently, first on one eye and then the other. She looked up at him and reached out to him.

"Johnny's here," he said.

She pushed herself up on her elbows. She was tanned a lovely golden color. "Gosh, have we slept till eleven?"

"It's only six o'clock," he said. "He seems to be in some kind of trouble."

"You want me to slip away to my place?"

"No. Turn up for breakfast when you feel like it. Back way. Sleep it out."

He kissed her, climbed out of bed, and walked, naked, into the bathroom. He stood for a moment under the needle-spray shower, dried himself, and walked into the dressing room. He pulled on a clean pair of underdrawers, a pair of tan slacks, and a pink knit sports shirt. He slipped his feet into a pair of sandals, brushed his hair into shape, and went down the winding staircase to the first floor.

Quist's living room was nothing at all like the simple

15

second floor. The walls were literally covered with photographs of famous people, autographed to Quist; there were movie stars and stage celebrities, famous politicians including a President of the United States, famous tycoons, and a few friends he loved who were not famous at all. There was, for example, a portrait in oils by the famous artist Gordon Stevenson of the girl who slept in the big bed upstairs. The furniture was very mod, unexpectedly comfortable. There was a bar at one end of the room. Guests rarely saw more than this room and the terrace. There was a study, austere by comparison, and elaborately efficient kitchen, and a small dining room, rarely used.

Quist stopped at a silver box on a stretcher table, took out a very long, very thin cigar, lit it with a silver table lighter, and went to the front door.

Johnny Sands stood outside in the hall, and Quist was shocked at the sight of him. The enormous vitality that exuded from the singer earlier in the evening had evaporated. He looked, somehow, small and shrunken. His eyes were glassy. He was sucking on a cigarette as though it would by some means give him life. He had changed from his dinner jacket to a brown tropical worsted suit with a yellow turtle-necked sweater.

"You took your time, pal," he said, and came in. Without another word to Quist he crossed the room to the bar, selected a bottle of Jamieson's Irish, and poured himself a staggering drink which he tossed off like water.

Quist sat down in a comfortable armchair, his pale eyes narrowed against the smoke from his cigar. "You want to sit or prowl?" he asked.

"Why don't you ask me what's life or death?" Johnny asked.

"Tell it your own way—from the beginning, if it isn't too much trouble," Quist said.

16

Johnny poured himself another drink, but this one he sipped as he began to move restlessly about. He looked up the winding staircase toward the second floor.

"Your babe's upstairs, I suppose," he said. "Not that it matters. You'd tell her anyway, even if I swore you to secrecy. Right?"

"Right," Quist said.

"Why didn't I ever find a girl like that," Johnny said.

"You have to be enormously lucky."

"You never bothered to marry her, did you?"

"That's really not any of your business, Johnny."

"Just curious, pal. My trouble is I married a lot of them, always the wrong ones."

Quist watched him, moving around, a tired old man caught up in some kind of anguish. "Life and death you said, Johnny."

"Oh, brother!" A cigarette out, a cigarette lit. "You read this morning's paper or hear the radio?"

"No."

"There was more to last night than no bomb on that plane."

"Oh?"

"A guy was shot to death in the washroom at the Chicago airport."

"Brian Marr mentioned something about it."

"I knew that guy."

Quist's eyebrows lifted. "The one who was shot?"

"Yes, I knew him. And like today or tomorrow someone may come up with the idea that I might have had a reason to finish him off."

"Did you?"

"God sake no, pal!"

Johnny took a long swallow of his drink. "Reason I changed things last night—about talking to you after the show—was I heard from a friend who had to see me.

17

Message came to the Garden. Reason I thought I ought to see him was that this friend also knew the guy who was shot to death in Chicago."

"So you saw him."

"So I *didn't* see him," Johnny said. He exhaled a lung full of smoke. "He was supposed to come to my hotel after the show. He never got there."

"Changed his mind?"

"No. He didn't change his mind. It got changed for him. He was run down by a hit-and-run driver, a block from my hotel, about four this morning. Dead. Very goddam stone dead."

"Two in one night."

"Yeah."

"Well, no one can tie you into this second one—can they?"

"I'll make you a bet they can."

"How?"

"God knows. But if they couldn't they wouldn't have killed him."

" 'They'? Who are 'they,' Johnny?"

"I wish I knew," Johnny said.

Quist flicked the ash from his cigar into a brass tray at his elbow. His lips moved in a faint smile. "You like to lie down on the couch?" he asked. "Feeling guilty about two murders you didn't commit sounds like work for a psychiatrist. Let Dr. Quist listen to your free associations, little man."

"Drop dead," Johnny said.

"I'd just as soon go back to bed if you're not going to tell me what it's all about, Johnny."

Back to the bar. Another drink. Another cigarette.

"It started five years ago," Johnny said. "A girl committed suicide."

"How?"

"Pills. Liquor. They don't mix, you know. Point is, she did it in my house in Beverly Hills." A nerve twitched high up on Johnny's cheek. He kept turned away from Quist.

"Nothing that happens to you stays out of the news," Quist said. "How come I never heard of this?"

"That's what it's all about," Johnny said. He moved over to the French doors opening onto the terrace and looked out at the river. "Her name was Beverly Trent—at least that was her show business name, named herself after the town, for God sakes." Johnny turned and grinned at Quist. "She made Raquel Welch look like Twiggy. A dish."

"One of your harem?"

"Well, you could say that, I suppose."

"So could I, or couldn't I?"

"We had a passage or two," Johnny said. "She wasn't the great passion of my life, even for ten minutes. Too obvious. No techniques. But I—well, I was either the great love of her life or the richest man she'd ever hooked up with in the hay. Either way she wanted me for keeps. She bored me. I told her to split and stay split. She had hysterics, phoned me in the middle of the night, showed up at the studio where I was working, at restaurants where I was eating. She made a hundred scenes. And, finally, she came to a party to which she wasn't invited and killed herself in my bed!"

"Without assistance from you?"

"You son of a bitch," Johnny said.

"Anything to get you to tell the story," Quist said. His cigar had gone out. He looked at it, frowning, and put it down in the ashtray.

"Like I said, I threw a party," Johnny said. "It was an impulse—spur of the moment thing. Somebody said champagne wasn't really an alcoholic drink; just sparkling water. You could drink it forever, they said. So I offered to provide all the champagne there was. Last one on his or her feet would win the prize—a thousand bucks to play with at the roulette tables in Las Vegas. About twenty guys and gals turned up to find out how watery champagne really is. Only rule was we poured a round, and everybody had to drink up before we poured a second round. Some of them went the way of all flesh pretty fast." Johnny chuckled at the memory. "It was a pleasant, congenial crowd until about halfway through. Then Beverly showed up. She was already potted, screaming her outrage at not having been invited. I told her to scram, but it was no dice. Rather than play the scene forever I added a good slug of brandy to her champagne. After two rounds of that she staggered out. I thought she was going to be sick, but she didn't come back, so I guessed we were just lucky.

"The party went on till daylight. A nice little chick who was playing in some TV series was the last one alive. I gave her a nice crisp one-thousand-dollar bill, put her in a taxi, and sent her home. I was pooped. I walked through the party wreckage and up to my room. There was Beverly, stark naked in my bed. Out cold, I thought. I was burned. Her clothes were tossed around on the chairs and on the floor. Her purse was spilled out on the bedside table and I noticed an empty pill bottle. When I went over to see what it was I saw that it was resting on top of a scrawled note. The note said: 'This is the only way I can be sure of being a part of your life forever.'

"I was suddenly scared. I tried to find a pulse beat. There wasn't any. She was dead. The pill bottle had contained maybe fifty sleeping pills. God knows how many she took—enough to kill a horse the coroner said later."

"Coroner? It got to the police?" Quist asked.

"Jesus, pal, unless you've lived my kind of life you wouldn't understand how I reacted. I didn't care for that girl. Alive, she'd been an interesting body, dead she was a terrifying body. I'd just finished a picture—*Glory Trail*, remember? It's the one in which I played a Catholic priest. I had a million bucks of my own money in that film. I was trying to create a new image in my declining years—kindly old Johnny Sands. I could see the headlines. 'Johnny Sands stages orgy. Girl suicide. Former girl friend—et cetera, et cetera.' Great for my Catholic priest; great for my new image. Little Beverly was going to be a part of my life forever all right!

"What I did, pal, was to protect myself. I had a couple of friends I knew I could trust. One was a guy named Louie Sabol, a Hollywood agent who was making a commission off me; the other was Max Liebman, a lawyer who handled some non-show-business deals for me. I could trust them because they were friends, also depending on me for the best part of their bread and butter. They came and we tried to figure out what to do. It seemed simple enough. We got some clothes on Beverly and we carried her out to a car, upright, like we were supporting a drunk. If anybody saw us they'd think we were just helping someone who'd had a few too many. We took her to her apartment in Los Angeles. It was about five o'clock in the morning, not many people stirring. Sunday morning. We were in luck. We let ourselves into her apartment with her key, laid her out on the bed, left the empty pill bottle beside her and took off.

"It was twenty-four hours before someone found her. It was pronounced a suicide—and of course it *was* a suicide. Nobody came forward to say they'd seen her brought home. Even if they had we weren't in too bad trouble. She'd passed out at a party; we'd brought her home. We didn't have to say that, so we didn't. We were home free!

A cop did come to see me. Someone at the party had mentioned she'd been there. I told him she'd come potted, left after a little. That, I told him, was all I knew. He was a right kind of guy. He knew what publicity would do to me, and there was no crime involved."

"Did you pay him off?" Quist asked.

"I was able to do him a few favors," Johnny said, unabashed.

"So?"

"So that was that—for about a year. Then it started. A phone call from a guy with a disguised voice. He knew everything about the whole mess, from A to Z. He knew about the note, even—and nobody knew about that but me, and Louie, and Max, and Beverly who was dead. But this guy knew."

"Blackmail?"

"Right. Like solid—like big. A hundred grand a year for two years."

"Wow!"

Johnny shook his head from side to side. His smile was weary. "You can say that again, pal. You know, from the day it began I knew I had a choice. Either I told this joker to go screw and face the public scandal, or I let myself be bled to death for the rest of my life. So, now you know why I retired two years ago."

"You stopped paying?"

"Cold."

"But there's been no scandal."

"Not so far," Johnny said, his voice grim. "Oh, he screamed and yelled and threatened."

"You still didn't have any lead to who he is?"

"No."

"How did you make the payments?"

"Cash. You won't believe it, but the money was left in the top drawer of the desk in my own house. When there

22

was no one there it was picked up. Oh, I tried watching for him, but he never showed up while I was watching. The money would stay there for days—until the place wasn't watched. So I quit." Johnny crunched out his cigarette in an ashtray and lit a fresh one. His hands weren't steady. "Then I was asked to do this benefit for Respiratory Diseases." The tired eyes were suddenly bright. "You know what it's like to give up something you've done and loved all your life, Julian? God damn I love to sing! And I'm still good, still the best. That's not vanity. I know. I started dreaming of that crowd in Madison Square Garden. It would be a ball. It would make me feel good again, young again. So I said I would. The publicity started with your help. I cut down on the booze and the butts, and I started working out in the gym. I can still run your tail off on the squash court, pal."

"Try me sometime," Quist said. He reached for his dead cigar and relit it. "You're going to tell me you heard from your blackmailing friend again."

Johnny nodded. "Cancel my part in the benefit or else. So I told him go ahead with his or else. I wasn't making a buck out of this. I was helping sick people. If he started a scandal about me I would still draw people. 'You go ahead with it,' he told me, 'and you'll wish you'd never been born.' I told him to go to hell, and I waited for him to spill the story. Nothing. Then, on the plane out of Chicago tonight the word that there might be a bomb on board. I damn near died right there, Julian. I knew it was for me."

"Except there wasn't one."

"Right. Then I figured my man had false-alarmed the bomb so that I couldn't make the benefit."

"Could be," Quist said.

Johnny's cigarette bobbed up and down between his lips as he spoke. He was suddenly gripping the back of a chair as if he needed to support himself. "We got back to the airport in Chicago."

" 'We'?

"Eddie was with me, of course. You know Eddie Wismer, my go-for? Been with me twenty-five years. Eddie was trying to make arrangements for me to get another flight, trying to reach you on the phone. It was while I was waiting that the word went through the terminal that some guy had been shot to death in the men's room." Johnny drew a deep breath. "It was Louie Sabol, the Hollywood agent who'd helped me that night with Beverly Trent."

Quist's pale eyes were narrowed, fixed on Johnny. "And the hit-and-run victim this morning was your lawyer friend, Max Liebman?" he asked softly.

Johnny nodded. "So it looks like I'm Center Stage, wouldn't you say?"

Chapter 3

THE FRONT DOOR bell sounded.

Quist got up and went to open it. Only four people in the world could get to that door without being preannounced by the lobby watchdogs. They were Lydia Morton; his private secretary Constance Parmalee; Dan Garvey and Bobby Hilliard, his two top assistants and associates in the business.

Lydia was outside the door, an amused twinkle in her dark violet eyes. She looked fresh and lovely in a simple cotton print.

"Thought maybe I could interest you in an earlier breakfast," she said. "I couldn't sleep." She came in, waved to Johnny who was at the bar.

"Hi, Lydia," Johnny said. He grinned at her. "You ever dream of being an actress?"

"I suppose I must have at some point," she said.

"Abandon the idea," Johnny said. "Your entrance was good, but it didn't ring true. You came down the back stairs from up above." He pointed.

"Julian told you," Lydia said, undisturbed.

"Maybe. But I knew anyway. I have a special radar system for special dolls. In spite of all the booze and butts maybe I smelled you. Like wildflowers, kiddo. Does he ever give you a night off?"

"Never," Lydia said.

"Well, if he ever does, just remember I'm the first one in line outside your door."

"That's the best offer I've had this morning," Lydia said.

"Oh boy, why didn't I get to you first," Johnny said, and reached for the bottle of Irish.

"Make some coffee, will you, doll?" Quist said. "And close the kitchen door while you're about it. Johnny and I have a few things to say in private before we decide whether you do or do not get into the act."

Lydia went out to the kitchen. Johnny watched her go.

"She's so damned lovely," he said.

Quist took a fresh cigar from the silver box on the table. "Question number one," he said. "Why are you here, Johnny, instead of at the local police precinct house? Why me and not the cops?" He lit his cigar.

Johnny started to roam again, glass in hand. "Sooner or later we all have to take a trip somewhere," he said. "Like heaven, or hell, or limbo. So help me, I can't get interested in it. I don't want to become dead."

"So ask the cops to protect you."

Johnny drew a deep breath. "Who called the airline to say there was a bomb on my plane? Anonymous. But it brought me back to the airport so I was there when Louie was shot. What was Louie doing in Chicago and at the airport? I don't know. What was Max Liebman doing in New York? I don't know. He was going to tell me. The Benefit Committee had hired a rent-a-car for me. I drove back from the Garden to my hotel in it this morning. I parked it and gave the key to the doorman at the hotel. That was about fifteen minutes before Max was found dead on the street. No one saw the accident. I could have

26

run him down, and I'll bet you four to one that there'll be something about that rented car that will suggest I did have some kind of an accident. I go to the cops and they'll be tipped off I had opportunity and maybe motive."

"What motive?"

"So it all comes out, pal, through my blackmailing friend. I covered up the true facts about Beverly's death. I paid two hundred grand to keep it hushed up. The two guys who knew the truth about it are dead. Maybe I thought one of them was the blackmailer and got rid of them both to be sure."

"Did you think one of them was the blackmailer?"

"Never occurred to me. Those guys were friends." Johnny's mouth was a straight, hard line. "I am fifty-eight years old, pal. I can look forward to a grand jury hearing, maybe an indictment. Then a trial, going on and on. Everything about my life will come out; Beverly, my four wives, dozens of other dames, God knows what else. Maybe I am convicted and go to jail while my expensive lawyers appeal. Maybe they make it, maybe they don't. I don't want to go through it, Julian. I can't go through it. I'd just as soon step off your terrace out there as go through it. I want to live; I want to do my thing and screw my blackmailing pal. I want to have fun. I could face the story about Beverly becoming public. If Louie and Max were here to back me up, I wouldn't look too bad. I'm not playing a Catholic priest anymore. Now there'll be hints of three murders, for God sake. I can't go through it, Julian."

"So you don't go to the cops. Then your blackmailing friend spills the beans anyway. No?"

"He may wait a little while to see what I do—a few hours, a few days, a few weeks. Maybe we can hit him

27

before he hits us."

"Wasn't Eddie Wismer with you? He's always with you?"

"He stayed behind at the Garden so he could help check out what we took."

"Johnny, I run a public relations business not a detective agency," Quist said.

"You've got people who are ten times smarter than private dicks," Johnny said. "You know the world I live in. I'm your client. If you try to dig up stuff about me, it won't seem out of the way. You have contacts with the press, radio, TV people. You can fight any kind of a gossip war that might start better than anyone else. You might keep my life livable for me, Julian. The cops can't and won't."

Quist was frowning. "If I agreed, Johnny, there are at least four people who would have to know the whole story. You'd have to risk that.

"Who are they?"

Quist nodded toward the kitchen. "Lydia—not because she's close to me, but because she's a key member of my staff. Dan Garvey who is my top man. Bobby Hilliard, whom you met at the Garden tonight. My personal secretary, Connie Parmalee. You've met her too, I think."

"Your ball game. You play it your way," Johnny said.

"I ought to have my head examined," Quist said. "But you're my friend, and my client."

Johnny's face broke into a broad grin. "I love you," he said.

The offices of Julian Quist Associates, high above Grand Central Station, were as mod as the rather gaudy clothes worn by their proprietor. The colors in the reception room were pale pastels, like Quist's bedroom. The furniture augured discomfort until you sat down in it, or on it, and discovered that it was delightfully comfortable. The walls usually displayed some very modern paintings, but they were changed at frequent intervals. On the Monday morning after Johnny Sands' benefit at the Garden the artists represented were Roy Lichtenstein, Larry Bell, and Don Eddy, all very much "with it."

Not that the paintings mattered very much to the people who passed through the reception room to one of the inner sanctums or to the elaborate waiting room for special clients. If you get as far as the waiting room it means you have a chance of being seen. The reason the paintings are, by and large, ignored is Miss Gloria Chard, the receptionist. Gloria sits in the center of a circular desk, juggling telephones, wearing a simple little Rudi Gernreich creation, looking as if she had been designed and put together by some kind of genius in the art of female allure. Mailmen deliver letters to the wrong office just to get a look at Miss Gloria Chard; delivery boys bring milkshakes and sandwiches to the wrong place on purpose; Miss Chard says "no" in her sexy voice more often than any other known female. She would almost certainly have said "yes" to one or two men in the office if asked, and there was something almost wistful about the way she eyed her boss.

Quist came in on that Monday morning a little before ten.

"Hello, darling," he said, entirely too casual to raise Miss Chard's hopes. "I have beriberi today so I can't see anyone but Dan, Lydia, and Bobby. Tell them now, will you, my pet?"

"There are a dozen urgent calls for you to return," Gloria said, "and Dr. Latham is waiting for you in the next room."

"Tell him tomorrow," Quist said. "The only client I'll talk to is Johnny Sands. Put him through directly if he calls."

"I hear he was great," Gloria said. "According to the paper they raised a million, two hundred and forty thousand dollars."

"Johnny earned it," Quist said.

Quist, wearing a double-breasted pale blue tropical worsted suit, walked down the corridor and into his private office. As he went in, another door at the far end of the room opened and Miss Constance Parmalee, his private secretary, stood there. She was a slim girl with a good figure, red hair, and the proper legs for the mini-skirt she was wearing. She had on amber-tinted granny glasses that shaded very bright, inquisitive hazel eyes.

"You and I are out for the day, darling," Quist said. "Dan and Lydia are on their way. Turn over the cannibals in the waiting room to someone bright, charming, and adamant. And haul in your stenotype machine."

"Dr. Latham is most insistent—"

"Tell him he can spend the day figuring out how to perform a brain transplant," Quist said. "I'll see him tomorrow. He should call at the end of the day for an exact time."

"You have a lunch date with Jud Walker."

"Cancel it. I love him. I grieve. We'll do it next week."

Miss Parmalee evaporated. Quist only had time to hang his jacket in a corner closet, select a long, thin cigar from a cedar-lined box on his desk, and light it with a silver desk lighter when Dan Garvey and Lydia Morton appeared. Lydia never arrived at or left the office with Quist. She had her own apartment a short two blocks from Quist's Beekman Place establishment. There was nothing in her manner that remotely suggested that she'd had breakfast with Quist two hours ago.

Dan Garvey is the complete physical opposite of Quist; dark, brooding, conservative as to clothes. They are both a little over six feet tall, but Garvey must weigh forty pounds more, not an ounce of it fat. He had been a promising professional football player when a knee injury cut his career short. He was good-looking enough to have had a career in films if he hadn't gone to work for Julian Quist Associates. He is just the man to have in your corner if the action gets physical. Hidden away among his private treasures is a Phi Beta Kappa key, which he has never mentioned to anyone.

Miss Parmalee reappeared with her stenotype machine and set herself up by Quist's desk.

"Good morning, class," Quist said. "The subject of today's lecture is confidential, strictly on the Q.T., off the record. I don't want a transcript from you, Connie. Just the essential facts so that we will have a reference file. It will be kept separate from any routine material we have on Johnny Sands."

"We are going to discuss Johnny Sands?" Garvey asked.

"We are."

"So we congratulate ourselves and go back to work," Garvey said. "We did a hell of a job for him. According to the morning paper he raised over a million and a quarter Saturday night."

"Paper tell you anything else, Daniel?"

"He sang till three-thirty in the morning."

"He was late because of a false bomb threat on the plane he took from Chicago," Lydia said. Nothing suggested that she'd spent most of Sunday with Quist and Johnny and discussed the whole situation far into the night.

"Good girl," Quist said.

Miss Parmalee looked up from the stenotype machine.

"An agent who handled some of Johnny's affairs in Hollywood was shot to death in the men's room at the Chicago terminal," she said. "I recognized the name from our files —Louis Sabol."

"A plus," Quist said.

"I contacted him about a month ago when we were preparing a bio on Johnny for the benefit," Miss Parmalee said.

"Any other interesting items in the paper that might relate to Johnny?"

"There are seven million people in the Los Angeles area," Garvey said. "If you assume that the great Johnny Sands has a connection with all of them, then there was an item on the short wave police radio yesterday. A Hollywood lawyer named Max Liebman was killed by a hit-and-run driver on Madison Avenue about four o'clock on Sunday morning."

"I'll complete the connection for you, Daniel, by telling you that Max Liebman was a good friend of Johnny's. Johnny's friends had a rough Saturday night and Sunday morning."

"So?" Garvey said.

"So listen," Quist said. He began to talk and Miss Parmalee's fingers moved on the stenotype machine. He told them the whole Johnny Sands story from top to bottom. Garvey, scowling, moved restlessly around the office as Quist unwound his tale.

"—and so," Quist said, when he had come to the end, "Johnny has asked me to help him."

"You want advice?" Garvey asked, his voice angry.

"No, Daniel. I want information. I want to know what brought Louis Sabol to the Chicago airport at the precise time that Johnny was there. I want to know what brought Max Liebman to New York, calling Johnny to tell him that he must see him. I want to know if there is any damage to Johnny's rent-a-car that would suggest he hit someone. I want to find out what there is to find out about the cop who kept things quiet for Johnny after Beverly Trent's death five years ago. I want to know who was at that champagne party. Johnny can only remember about a dozen of them. His life has been too full of parties. Eddie Wismer, his go-for, can probably produce a guest list."

"Go-for?" Miss Parmalee asked.

"Go for a cup of coffee, go for a sandwich, go for an airplane ticket," Garvey said. "Go for whatever I want or need." He glared at Quist. "You still don't want advice?"

Quist smiled. "You're going to give it whether I want it or not."

"Somewhere there is a long-lost brother, father, boy friend of the late Miss Beverly Trent's," Garvey began.

"Excuse me, Daniel," Quist said. He gestured to Miss Parmalee. "Beverly Trent was a show business name, not the lady's real moniker. We need to find out what her real name is and if she has a long-lost brother, father, boy friend."

Miss Parmalee's fingers moved.

"Some nut like that is the blackmailer," Garvey said. "Since the money has dried up he has now become the god of vengeance. He got Sabol, he got Liebman, he'll get Johnny—unless you get in the way and he gets you first, Julian. My advice is persuade Johnny to go to the cops, and if he won't, let him paddle his own canoe. You're not a Mannix. Johnny may be your friend, but that doesn't require you to put your own survival on the line."

"Did anyone ever tell you, Daniel, that you look like Mike Connors?" Quist asked cheerfully.

"Who the hell is Mike Connors?"

"The actor who plays Mannix on television."

"Drop dead," Garvey said.

33

"That would be contrary to your advice, Daniel." Quist leaned forward to put the stub of his cigar down in the ashtray. "I want answers to the questions I've set up. I need them like yesterday. I expect them by tomorrow."

There was silence.

"Johnny knows that you three people have the whole rundown," Quist said. "He'll help in any way he can. I think you ought to hop a jet for Hollywood, Daniel. That's the starting point for the cop, for Sabol, for Liebman. Lydia and I will work this end. I'll expect a full report from you tomorrow night."

"What I ought to do is find a padded cell and lock you in it," Garvey said.

"When you report back and show me I'm in over my head I'll surrender," Quist said. "I'd like it if we could move quickly and efficiently. I don't want to be trying to solve this thing after Johnny is in the morgue."

Chapter 4

Mrs. DELBERT SCHEER, the working chairman of the Foundation to Combat Respiratory Diseases, lived in a beautifully remodeled brownstone house in the East Eighties. The keynote was simple elegance. Standing in a small reception room at the street level of the house Quist told himself that the Scheers were not new rich. The rug was Turkish, a museum piece. The two high-backed chairs and the square center table on which a little silver dish for calling cards rested were probably the work of a Florentine artisan of an earlier century. There was a portrait in oil of a hard-faced gentleman, a brass plate informing the world that this was Delbert Scheer. Quist wondered if he was the lady's husband or her father-in-law. He looked in his sixties, considerably older than the lady he'd seen at the Garden on Saturday night. A date under an indistinguishable artist's signature indicated the portrait had been painted ten years ago.

The maid, uniformed, who had admitted Quist returned to tell him that Mrs. Scheer would be delighted to see him in her private sitting room on the third floor. She led him to a small, old-fashioned elevator and pressed the button marked "3" for him.

The private sitting room was bright with sunshine.

Again, the taste was impeccable. Mrs. Scheer, herself, was something of a surprise to Quist. On Saturday night she had been overdressed, overjeweled. Today she wore a very simple, very expensive, wool dress, no jewelry except a broad gold wedding band on her finger. She was younger than he had thought, not more than early forties. Her figure was astonishingly good, almost youthful. She moved briskly, a hand held out to him.

"What a delightful surprise," she said. Her handshake was firm. "You may not believe it, but I have been trying to reach you on the phone this morning, Mr. Quist."

"I've been out of my office," he said.

"Do sit down," she said. "Is it too early in the day for a drink, or would you prefer some coffee?"

"Nothing, thanks very much," Quist said. He took the comfortable armchair she indicated.

"I wanted to thank you for the marvelous way you handled things on Saturday night," Marian Scheer said. "Without you I think we'd all have had a nervous breakdown and abandoned ship."

"It was Johnny who made it work."

"Wasn't he marvelous!"

"There's no one quite like him," Quist said.

Marian Scheer sat down facing him, her smile questioning him.

"That's an interesting portrait of your husband in the reception room downstairs," Quist said. "It is of your husband, isn't it?"

"Yes."

"Was he at the Garden on Saturday night?"

Her smile didn't waver. "My husband died about six years ago, Mr. Quist."

"Sorry to have been clumsy."

"Not at all," she said. "Delbert lived a very full, active life. He was seventy-two when he died on the way to his office one morning."

So she had been something more than thirty years younger than her husband. Her interest in Quist, simply as a male, was not abnormal. He felt it strongly. She was ready for adventure, Quist told himself.

"I wanted to ask you a question," Quist said, "which you may find rather odd."

"I'll do my best with it," she said.

"Was any effort made to dissuade your committee from having Johnny perform at your benefit?"

Her expertly penciled eyebrows rose. "Good Lord, no. Why should there have been?"

"You know that I handle Johnny's public relations work," Quist said. "Someone has been trying to make trouble for him."

"Who?"

"I wish I knew," Quist said. "People who reach Johnny's kind of public position are often the targets for crackpots, anonymous letter writers, psychotic troublemakers. In my business I come across this kind of thing constantly—a harassment by idiots. I'm inclined to think the phony bomb alarm on Johnny's plane Saturday night came from that kind of source—someone trying to keep him from appearing, trying to damage his public image." Quist smiled. "It's my job to keep that image bright and shining. I wondered if anything had come your way to discredit him or to persuade you not to have him for the benefit."

"What a miserable thing for anyone to do," Marian Scheer said. She took a cigarette from a box on the table beside her chair. "Please smoke if you care to, Mr. Quist."

"I'm afraid I'm a cigar smoker."

"I love the smell of cigars," she said.

He rose and held his lighter for her cigarette. From the inside pocket of his jacket he took a thin leather case and produced one of his cigars.

"How awful for Johnny," Marian Scheer said.

"A constant series of threats, endless abuse, is the main reason why Johnny retired two years ago," Quist said, stretching the truth. "Saturday night he showed us what a loss he is to the entertainment world. I'd like to put a stop to his tormentor if I could, because I'd like to see him pick up his career again."

"I'm really shocked by what you're saying, Mr. Quist. No, nothing came to the committee to suggest anyone thought we shouldn't use Johnny."

"How did you happen to get Johnny for your evening? He'd announced he'd never do a public performance again."

"Why the idea came from him," Marian Scheer said. "Didn't you know? Some years ago he did a benefit for the Foundation in Las Vegas. When it was announced that we were staging our main function this year at Madison Square Garden, Johnny telephoned me from Hollywood. He said he thought he might still be able to attract an audience, 'shake them loose from a little bread' is the phrase he used. Of course I was ecstatic. We couldn't have had a bigger draw anywhere. He agreed to be nominal chairman of the fund-raising committee. He promised us your help and your nice Mr. Hilliard was marvelous."

"You knew Johnny, then?"

"I wasn't involved with the Foundation when he did the Las Vegas show," she said. "I didn't know him personally. He called me because I was listed as chairman. I couldn't have been happier."

"I can imagine. And no one tried to put a spoke in the wheel?"

"No."

Quist smiled. "I had hoped," he said. "I need a lead, badly. One other question, Mrs. Scheer." He proceeded blandly to twist the truth a little further. "I understand your committee rented a car for Johnny. Can you tell me from whom you rented it? You see, someone left a threatening note for Johnny in it."

"My God, Mr. Quist! The details were handled by the Foundation secretary. Let me call her."

"I'd appreciate it."

Marian Scheer got up from her chair and went quickly out of the room. Quist stood and then wandered over toward a desk in the corner. He had noticed a large photograph in a silver frame as he'd talked to his hostess. It was a picture of Marian Scheer in a wedding gown, her white gloved hand slipped through the arm of Delbert Scheer, looking like her grandfather. She had been maturely lovely in the picture. Someone had written a date in the corner of the picture—May 12, 1962. Maid Marian, he thought, had not had Delbert Scheer for long if he had died six years ago. The old gentleman had obviously left her very well off, which must have been a compensation.

She rejoined him, holding a little slip of paper in her hand. "The East River Car Rental Garage," she said, handing him the paper.

"Coincidence," he said. "I keep my own car in their garage. Well, thank you so much for letting me take up your time, Mrs. Scheer."

"Marian, please," she said. "Could I persuade you to stay for lunch with me? There's no one else."

Quist expressed regrets. It might have been interesting, he thought. The lady was awfully hungry—but not for lunch.

"But you will come to my party," she said.

"Party?"

"Oh dear, you don't know about it, do you? That's what I was trying to call you about this morning—Julian. I'm giving a party for Johnny here tomorrow night. A few members of the committee who will enjoy something informal. Johnny's bringing a girl friend of his. Buffet supper at seven. Drinks before and after. Johnny may even sing for us."

"Well, I—"

"If you'd care to bring that lovely girl who was with you on Saturday night she'd be most welcome." She was standing very close to him now, her hand resting on his arm.

"I think Miss Morton and I would like very much to come," Quist said, wondering who Johnny's girl friend was. "Informal, you say?"

"Johnny loathes to dress for anything. He wears dinner clothes at his work. He likes to be informal at play."

"You've gotten to know him quite well in a couple of days," Quist said.

Color rose in her cheeks. "Oh, he came East about a month ago to finalize the arrangements. But you know that, of course."

Johnny, Johnny, Quist thought, no one is safe from you. But perhaps no one wants to be!

"Tomorrow at seven then—Marian," he said.

"Dear Julian, you've made my party for me," she said, and gave his arm a little squeeze.

"You should have phoned if you wanted your car, Mr. Quist," the garage attendant said. "It'll take me a little while to dig it out."

"No sweat, Tommy," Quist said. "I don't want the car." They were standing on the sidewalk outside the East River Car Rental Garage. "I wanted to ask you a question about the rental business."

"Shoot."

"How carefully do you check a car before the renter takes it out?"

"Stem to stern," Tommy said. "Have to for insurance reasons. Fellow comes back with a stoved-in fender and tells us it was that way when he took it out. We have a record of just what condition it was really in when he took it."

"I imagined. A client of mine, Johnny Sands, rented a car from you on Saturday. Could you check to see what shape it was in?"

Tommy laughed. "I can tell you without checking, Mr. Quist. It just happens I was the one who passed on it. Not my job as a rule, but I asked for it. My wife is nuts about Johnny Sands. I thought I might get his autograph for her. Trouble was he didn't come for the car himself. Some dame."

"Who?"

"Said she was secretary for the outfit Johnny was doing a benefit for Saturday night. Elizabeth Somebody—I forget. I could look it up for you."

"The car was taken in her name?"

"No, in Johnny Sands' name. Ordinarily we have to have a driver's license number and all that. We didn't need it for Johnny Sands. Everybody in the whole goddam world knows him."

"And the condition of the car?"

"Clean. Hound's tooth clean. We wouldn't want him driving around in a dented wreck."

"Thanks, Tommy. You want Johnny Sands' autograph I can get it for you."

"Oh brother, Mr. Quist. You get that for me and I'll have hash browned potatoes three nights running." He grinned. "My favorite way of cooking potatoes, which my old lady does only once a year."

"Count on it," Quist said.

He walked west and then down Lexington Avenue toward his office. The sunlight made his hair a bright, shining gold. People turned to look at the mod suit, worn with elegance. Normally it amused Quist to have people gawk at him, but on this occasion he seemed to be lost in thought, chin lowered, scowling. Before talking to his friend Tommy at East River Rental he had been to another garage, the one used by the hotel where Johnny was staying. He had looked at the rented car, and Johnny had been right. The right front fender and the right segment of the front bumper were dented. The car had been washed, so that anything that might have been of use to, say, the police laboratory, was gone. There would be no bloodstains, no pieces of hair or cloth. It turned out there was a kind of a routine about car washing. The doorman would ask if the owner wanted his car washed. It meant an extra buck for the nightman at the garage. Most people said "yes" without thinking about it. Johnny, the doorman remembered, had said, "Why not?" Casual. Not really listening, the doorman remembered. One thing was certain. If someone was trying to frame Johnny, the rented car would be very little use in its present state. The dents could have come from any sort of minor accident, or even the result of someone backing into the car in a parking space. There was nothing to tie it into a hit-and-run.

Gloria Chard gave Quist her dazzling smile as he came into the office.

"I've had six invitations to lunch and two to look at etchings tonight," she said. "That's what happens when you're 'out' for the day."

"Choose the most likely, love," Quist said.

"And Johnny Sands is in your office. My God, he's amazing. He looks thirty-five," Gloria said.

"You're due for your annual eye checkup," Quist said, and went down the corridor to his office.

Connie Parmalee was standing at attention in the doorway to her private room. It wasn't a psychic phenomena that had her always at the ready when Quist arrived. A buzzer between her desk and Gloria Chard's desk warned her in time.

Johnny was sitting in an aluminum-trimmed armchair, his head lolling to one side, sound asleep. On a table beside the chair was a half-empty bottle of liquor and an empty shot glass.

"After I had said 'no,' firmly, I had to send out for a bottle of Irish," Connie said. "He passed out quickly."

"Half a bottle isn't quick."

"The way he puts it down it is."

Without moving Johnny opened one eye. He smiled. "Passed out my foot," he said. He grinned at Connie. "I cleaned that up for you. When you get to be my age you learn to take forty winks whenever there isn't anything else to do." He sat up straight and reached for the bottle.

Quist made a small gesture to Connie and she disappeared. He walked over to his desk, selected one of his long, thin cigars, and sat down.

"As you predicted, your car is dented," he said, and lit his cigar.

"Oh God," Johnny said.

"But clean as far as a hit-and-run is concerned. You ordered it washed."

"The hell I did!"

The doorman asked you and you said, 'Why not?' "

"Maybe he did. I don't remember."

"No matter. Unless someone comes forward to claim he was an eyewitness the car won't hang you."

"Jesus, you really *are* a detective," Johnny said. "Which brings me to why I'm here."

"Free liquor, I thought."

"I'll send you a case of Irish. Twelve for one, that's the kind of guy I am." He sang softly, " *'I'm bidin' my time.*

43

That's the kind of guy I'm.' Serious-like. Your man Garvey called me a few hours back. On his way to California, he said, and what was the name of the cop I told you was decent to me when Beverly knocked herself off."

"So?"

"So I gave it to him, but afterwards I began to sweat and I couldn't get Garvey back. Look, pal, that cop—his name is Marshall—didn't cover up anything for me except that Beverly had been at my party before she went home and killed herself."

"Before she killed herself and you took her home."

"He doesn't know that. Ask him a lot of questions and he may begin to wonder. Your man Garvey could open a whole can of peas."

"Daniel can be trusted not to open up anything," Quist said.

"I hope to God."

Quist flicked the ash from his cigar. "I paid a visit to your girl friend, Mrs. Scheer."

Johnny exploded a laugh. "Girl friend!"

"She blushed at the very thought of you."

Johnny shook his head. "I am not a gentleman," he said. "I'm a kiss-and-tell kid. I wouldn't want to offend you, pal."

"Try me," Quist said, unsmiling.

"At my age—I guess it's true of anyone 'getting on,' as they say—my eye keeps wandering to younger and younger dames. They're more challenging and, in this day and age, more amiable. One thing I'd have sworn, after a somewhat purple lifetime, there was nothing anyone could teach me. I came East to work out details with the committee chairman—our gal Marian. I went to her luxurious palace on the East Side, armed with pencil, paper, a sheaf of notes. I wound up in a large, antique, four-poster bed on the third floor. I discovered my education had been incomplete. Would you believe that? I learned from her! Only trouble is, she's interested in permanence. Not me. You know someone who's looking for a lifetime of eroticism I'd be glad to write a letter of recommendation."

"But you're going to her party tomorrow."

"Surrounded by a bevy of beautiful dolls," Johnny said. "Self-protection. You going? She asked you, didn't she?"

"Surrounded by Lydia," Quist said.

"If I had Lydia I wouldn't go," Johnny said.

"You're not trying to save a friend from being knocked off, or charged with murder and hanged," Quist said.

"Sorry," Johnny said, his grin fading. "Sorry and grateful."

Eddie Wismer, constantly referred to as Johnny's "gofor," was, in his built-up shoes, about five feet three inches tall. He was chunky, strong-looking, with a belligerent, pug-nosed Irish face.

"I was born in a dressing room in an old vaudeville house in Cleveland," Eddie told Lydia Morton. "Somebody tied off my umbilical cord, plopped me in an old costume trunk, and my mother went out on stage with my father to do their act. Show must go on, and all that."

"I don't believe a word of it," Lydia said. She had only been half-listening. She and Julian had often come to the Beaumont Hotel. They'd had cocktails in the famous Trapeze Bar, gone to the Blue Lagoon Room after the theater to hear some top-flight performer do his or her thing, lunched in the grill; but she had never been in one of the rooms or suites. The top luxury hotel in the world. Johnny Sands' suite was perfection. It must, she thought, have been designed for him. The sitting room was furnished in heavy, masculine-looking stuff, paneled in a dark oak. There were half a dozen of Al Frueh's famous

45

theatrical caricatures on the walls—drawings of old-timers like DeWolf Hopper, Weber and Fields, Leo Dietrichstein, Willie Collier, George M. Cohan. There was a complete little bar with silver-topped bottles. Johnny might have furnished it himself.

Lydia's instructions from Quist had been specific. "Find an opportunity to talk to Eddie Wismer. He knows the whole story but he's seen it all with different eyes than Johnny's. He knows we know, that Johnny wants him to help. But I don't want Johnny prompting him."

The chance had come early that afternoon. Johnny had come to the office and settled in to wait for Quist. According to Connie Parmalee he would wait at least as long as it took him to drink a bottle of Jamieson's Irish whiskey. Lydia had called the Beaumont, gotten Eddie on the phone, and asked if she might drop in for a chat.

"I didn't know if I should come to Mr. Quist or if he'd set it up," Eddie said.

"I'm elected," Lydia told him.

"How lucky can I get?" Eddie asked with exaggerated gallantry.

He was waiting for her in the Beaumont's lobby. "We could go to one of the bars," he said, "but we could talk better in Johnny's place. If you're not afraid."

She looked down at him. Being a comfortable five feet seven she had to look down. "Afraid of what?"

"I might start chasing you around the living room table," he said.

"I'll risk it."

She was wearing dark blue slacks and a gray suede jacket over a man's white shirt. People turned to look at her as they crossed the lobby to the elevators. She had a kind of electricity that caught attention. She knew no way to turn it off.

Eddie settled her in a deep, red leather armchair and

46

brought her a Dubonnet on the rocks. He lit her cigarette
for her. Then he perched on the edge of a solid table and
grinned at her. From that position he was looking down
at her.

"I don't know what I can tell you that Johnny hasn't already told you," he said.

"You can tell me about Johnny," she said, "in a way he
wouldn't tell it."

His Irish face reflected love. "Johnny is the greatest,"
he said. "It started with me—jeese—twenty-five years ago.
Would you believe that? It seems like yesterday. He was
making a film, and I was working around the studio—
sweeping up, cleaning up." Eddie's face twisted. "I was in
vaudeville with my family almost as soon as I could walk.
Song-and-dance routines. My mother was the comic and
my father the straight man—I have to know now they
were a fifth-rate Burns and Allen. But there was vaudeville in almost every town over five thousand people in
the United States. Fifth-raters worked, until the movies
clobbered them to death. I used to sing patter songs, do a
soft-shoe, buck-and-wing. Then Mickey Rooney came
along and I was dead. Back in the days of 'The Hardy
Family' I tried to get a job as his stand-in. I wasn't even
good enough for that, I guess, even though I was about
the same size and even looked like him a little."

"You look like yourself, Eddie, nobody else," Lydia
said, crossing her long legs.

He looked at her like an adoring spaniel. "Thanks for
saying it," he said. "Well, anyway, I wound up on the
mop-up crew at the studio. One day Johnny—boy, did I
admire him—says, 'Hey, kiddo, get me a black coffee and
a package of butts, will yuh?' So I ran off to the commis-
sary and got him his coffee and cigarettes. I knew the
kind he smoked. I'd been watching him. He handed me a
five-dollar bill and told me to keep the change. I told him

47

'no,' I'd like him to let me do him a favor. He gave me a funny look and said, 'If you want to do me a favor, come around to my dressing room when the shooting's over.' So I went, and he asked me about myself, and I told him about the old vaudeville days, and we started telling each other some of the old jokes and laughing ourselves sick. All of a sudden he said, 'You want to do me a favor, work for me.' I asked him what I could do for him. 'Whatever I think up on the spur of the moment,' he said." Eddie shook his head in a kind of wonder. "And that's the way it's been for twenty-five years."

Lydia wondered how long it would take Johnny to finish a bottle of Irish. She had to get to the point. "You know why I'm here, Eddie. Johnny's asked Mr. Quist to help him."

"Oh God, I'm so scared for him, Miss Morton. Some sonofabitch—excuse me—is out to get him."

"Tell me about the champagne party where it all started, Eddie."

He shook his head again form side to side. "Would you believe, Miss Morton, that the one time he needed me real bad I wasn't there? There was a girl he'd been making a big play for." Eddie grinned. "He's always making a big play for some doll, you know. This girl and Johnny had some sort of a squabble and she'd high-tailed it off to Acapulco. Johnny sent me after her, with letters and a diamond bracelet, and some arguments. I was to be the Miles Standish to his John Alden."

Lydia smiled. "It's the other way around, Eddie. You were John Alden."

"Oh, yeah? Well, anyway, I was to try to make her feel good about him. He couldn't go himself. He had a recording session coming up the next morning. He made it, too, in spite of what happened. He made a big selling album that next morning. The point is, I wasn't there. If I had been, he wouldn't have had to call on Louie Sabol and Max Leibman. When I got back from Acapulco we waited around for days for the roof to cave in, but it didn't."

"How did you make out with the girl?"

"I didn't. That was a bad weekend for Johnny."

Lydia shifted in her chair and lit a fresh cigarette. "You knew Beverly Trent?"

"That bitch," Eddie said. "I knew she was trouble the first time I laid eyes on her. I warned Johnny. But she was built like Raquel Welch and he wanted to romp around with her. When he'd had it, she wasn't willing to give up. Made his life miserable."

"About the party, Eddie."

He took a cigarette out of his pocket, flipped it into the air, and caught it between his lips. He grinned at her. "Part of the old vaudeville routine," he said.

Lydia smiled back at him and clapped softly. He lit the cigarette with a match. "That party is about the only thing in Johnny's life for the last twenty-five years I haven't been a part of," he said. "Like I said, I was in Acapulco, being John Alden or Miles Standish, or whoever." There was a faraway look in his eyes as if he would like to tell about that. "The party wasn't planned, you understand. Johnny was eating and drinking at Chasen's with some of his pals. Somebody made this crack about champagne being no more than sparkling water. Johnny laughed at them and offered to buy all the champagne they could drink to test out the theory. He offered a prize of a thousand bucks to the last man alive. Right there in Chasen's they picked up a crowd and went back to Johnny's house."

"Could you tell me who all the people were, Eddie?"

"Not all," Eddie said. "Johnny and I tried to figure it out—after the trouble. I mean, he tried to remember, and

I tried to check it out with people who'd been there. We figured maybe somebody had slipped away to be sick, or pass out, and not left the house. That someone, if he stayed behind, could have known everything that happened. Johnny came up with a list of about fifteen or sixteen names, guys and dolls. But there were at least three or four others. They were strangers to Johnny. They just joined the parade out of Chasen's. We've never been able to put a name to them, and Johnny and the friends we asked couldn't really remember faces. A couple of guys, a couple of gals. Everybody got drunk very quick at that party." Eddie's smile was grim. "Champagne ain't sparkling water, you know. And belted down, a whole glass at a time—" He shrugged.

"It seems logical that somebody did stay behind, unknown to Johnny," Lydia said. "One thing that puzzled us was that, according to Johnny, the blackmailer knew about the note. It could only mean that he was in the room where Beverly Trent died. Johnny destroyed the note before he and his friends moved her. The blackmailer had to see it before that."

"Right," Eddie said.

"By the way, Eddie, what was Beverly Trent's real name? Johnny says 'Beverly Trent' was a show business name. Dan Garvey suggests the blackmailer could be some long-lost brother, father, boy friend of the girl's."

"Oh, we tried to check that out," Eddie said. "Her real name was Louise Hauptmann. She had no family we could ever find out about. Came out of an orphanage in Minnesota somewhere. German name—lot of German people in that area. Out of a soap opera. Left on the doorstep, name pinned to her bathrobe. Nobody in the area named Hauptmann. Got out when she was eighteen. Worked as a waitress and a hat-check girl in some booby trap in St. Paul. Won a beauty contest. Went to Hollywood to become a movie star." Eddie snorted. "With those buzzooms she had no trouble sleeping with a lot of agents and casting directors. Trouble was she couldn't act, couldn't sing or dance. Back to hat-check, where Johnny saw her. When she got to him she decided she wasn't ever going to let go. That's what it was all about."

Lydia was silent for a moment. Then: "Eddie, tell me about Saturday night. The bomb scare. And, by the way, what was Johnny doing in Chicago?"

Eddie's mouth tightened. "Stopover. Girl friend."

"He really has a chain of them, doesn't he?"

Eddie grinned. "Johnny's worked everywhere in the world in his time, and everywhere he worked there was a chick. In those early days there was only one town where he didn't make out with someone—Joplin, Missouri. Would you believe, after he was famous, he played Joplin for peanuts, just so there wouldn't be that black mark on his record?"

"Saturday night," Lydia prompted.

"So we stopped over in Chicago on the way from the Coast. Johnny saw his old flame and met me at the airport. We took off, and then the pilot notified us they'd been warned there might be a bomb on the plane and he was turning back. We sweat that one out. Brother. Soon as we were down I went to find out what other plane we could get out of there. Johnny went to phone Mr. Quist. It all took time. All of us were searched, all our luggage. While I was making arrangements I heard someone had been shot in the men's room. We didn't know who it was till we got to New York and heard it on the taxicab radio. Louie Sabol, for God sake! Old friend—and part of that champagne night. When we got to the Garden and Johnny was changing there was this phone call from Max Liebman. I suppose he'd heard about Louie. Johnny says he sounded hysterical; had to see him. Johnny told him to come here, to the Beaumont, when the benefit was over. He never came. Then we heard—about him."

"How?"

"Radio." He waved toward the set in the corner. "Next morning."

"Do you know what Sabol was doing in Chicago and Liebman in New York, Eddie?"

"Haven't the foggiest. But I'm scared as hell for Johnny. Looks like someone was trying to wipe out everyone connected with that night—the champagne party night."

"You think he ought to go to the police?"

"I understand why he doesn't want to," Eddie said. "If there's any chance of him coming back—and I know he thinks about it—the whole story would come out and wreck him. His friends would all begin to wonder about him. Some people might even start thinking he killed that Beverly bitch. It would wreck him, spoil all his fun. You people—you and Mr. Quist and all—might come up with the truth without starting a big scandal. I understand that. But you aren't equipped to protect Johnny the way the cops could. That's all that worries me about it."

"I think Julian feels the way you do," Lydia said, "but Johnny is a friend, and he pleaded a good case, Eddie."

Eddie smiled. "He could sell bikinis to the Eskimos."

"Well, thanks for your help, Eddie." Lydia put down her glass and snubbed out her cigarette. Eddie didn't move from his perch on the table.

"It would be less than polite, Miss Morton, if I didn't ask you if you'd be interested in a little love-making," he said.

She looked at him, her violet eyes widening.

He sounded bitter. "That's Johnny's technique," he said. "Of course some people say no, but on the other hand he gets an awful lot of love-making. Thanks, anyway, for not laughing."

"Laughing?" Her voice sounded odd to her.

"When a midget asks you to make love it's usually a joke. Nobody stops to think that just because I'm shrimp-sized I'm still a man!" His fists were clenched.

"It never occurred to me that you weren't, Eddie," Lydia said gently. "And thanks for asking. It makes me feel attractive. Unfortunately I'm a one-man woman, and at the moment I'm involved—very much involved."

"Lucky stiff," Eddie said.

A nice little man, Lydia thought, as she walked out through the Beaumont's lobby. A sad little man. A loyal little man, so loyal to Johnny Sands that it made her wonder if Johnny realized just what sort of friend he had in his go-for.

Monday passed. There was very little in the papers about the double murders of Louie Sabol and Max Lieb-man. They had either failed to make the connection between the dead men and Johnny Sands, or they didn't choose to make the connection until they had more facts. There was a great deal about the bomb scare on the plane and the fact that a show-biz celebrity had been one of the passengers. The warning to the airline, it seemed, had come by way of a telegram to the traffic manager at the airport. Attempts to trace the sender had drawn a blank. The telegram had been phoned in, charged to a number that turned out to be a phony. There had been an instruction not to deliver the wire until what turned out to be after the flight had taken off. A busy and per-haps stupid gal in the telegraph office had counted the words without consciously reading the message. She took hundreds a day and blacked out on most of them. In-structions were followed, the message delivered after the takeoff.

In a separate story the *News* reported that Louis Sabol, a Hollywood agent, had been shot to death in the men's room at the Chicago airport. Mr. Sabol's office reported that he had gone to Chicago "on business." Quist read it, frowning. The paper listed a number of Sabol's clients, TV and movie stars, but Johnny's name wasn't among them. It should have headed the list if, as Johnny had said, Sabol agented for him.

Liebman was buried somewhere on an inner page. A Los Angeles lawyer, victim of a hit-and-run driver in the early hours of the morning. Liebman was said to have been in New York "on business."

Quist had waited up quite late on Monday night, expecting to hear from Dan Garvey, but there was nothing. It wasn't until after he had arrived at the office on Tuesday morning that Dan made contact. Quist delayed accepting the person-to-person call until he'd gotten Lydia and Bobby Hilliard into his office along with Connie Parmalee.

When it was set up he let the call come in.

"Hi, Daniel. This is on the conference box, chum. Lydia, Bobby, and Connie are with me. Fire away."

Garvey's voice came through the amplifier on Quist's desk. "I couldn't call last night, Julian. Hadn't collected enough."

"Trip worth while?"

"You be the judge," Garvey said. "Connie ready?"

Quist glanced at Miss Parmalee who had set up her stenotype machine. "Fire away," he said.

"Out here we have number three," Garvey said.

"Number three what?"

"Number three dead man," Garvey said, his voice sounding harsh. "Marshall, the Hollywood cop."

"Dead?"

"And on the ripe side in this hot weather," Garvey said.

"I went looking for him first thing yesterday afternoon. It turns out he'd retired from the force; living in a little cottage near the ocean. When I got there I found three days' milk delivery outside the back door—three days of newspapers in his mailbox. Back door was open so I went in. What looked like Friday's breakfast half-eaten on the table. Electric percolator still plugged in. No Marshall. I felt uneasy, Julian."

"I can understand."

"Went to a neighbor's. This guy told me Marshall always took an early morning dip in the ocean. We went down a path to the beach. Marshall was there, skull bashed in. Not dressed for a swim; slacks and shirt, sneakers on his feet. Looked like a fall from the cliff, the neighbor thought."

"I thought—think—not," Garvey said. "He was lying in the sand, no rock nearby. Looked to me like he'd been hit half a dozen times. Cops are inclined to agree with me. The milk, the papers, indicate it must have happened Friday morning. Coroner thinks so too."

"And the finger points to—?"

"No one," Garvey said. "Blacktop driveway to the cottage so there are no tire marks of anyone's car. Neighbors didn't see anyone. Marshall's own car in the garage. So far, that's it."

Quist glanced at Lydia and Bobby Hilliard. They had no questions. "Go on, Daniel."

"I visited Sabol's office and Liebman's. Weeping secretaries. Black gloom. Same story in both places."

"What story?"

"Johnny asked Sabol to meet him in Chicago. Urgent. Johnny asked Liebman to meet him in New York. Urgent."

"For God sake, Dan, are you telling us—?"

"I swallowed hard myself," Garvey said. "But it comes

out queer. Same in both places. Johnny didn't call himself; didn't speak to either man as far as anyone knows. According to Sabol's secretary a man called. She assumed it was Eddie Wismer, although she admits he didn't give himself a name. He was calling for Johnny, he said. Johnny wanted Sabol to meet him at the Chicago airport —named the time. 'Tell Mr. Sabol,' the voice said, 'it's about some very special champagne.' The secretary knew Sabol couldn't go; he was up to there in work. But when she delivered the message Sabol turned green and ordered her to book him on a flight to Chicago."

"You say you got the same story at Liebman's office?"

"Right. Man didn't name himself; calling for Johnny Sands. Johnny wanted Liebman to meet him in New York right after the benefit at the Garden. Liebman was to call him at the Garden to name a time and place. The secretary didn't know if she could find Liebman. He was out playing golf with a client somewhere. The man said it was urgent. She was to tell Liebman it was about 'some very special champagne.' She located Liebman and he quit in the middle of his golf game and boarded a jet for Fun City."

"Did she, too, think the caller might be Eddie Wismer?"

"No." Garvey chuckled. "She didn't mention it so I asked. She blushed a nice girlish pink and said if it had been Eddie she'd have recognized his voice. I suspect she knows Eddie a little better than she cared to admit."

"Did the girls think the calls were local?"

"How would they know, Julian? You can dial direct from Hoboken these days and it sounds like you're next door. No operator in between. But my number one guess is the calls came from out in this area. Nobody knocked off Marshall, the cop, long distance. It adds up like this, Julian. Marshall was killed around breakfast time on Friday morning—whatever breakfast time was. The calls to the two others were made late Friday afternoon. There was plenty of time for our man to get to Chicago ahead of Sabol. Time for him to send a telegram to the control tower at the airport from a Chicago phone. Plenty of time after that for him to get to New York to take care of Liebman."

"And Johnny," Quist said.

"And you!" Garvey said. "Somebody wiping out everybody connected with the Trent case—and quite likely anyone who gets in the way. Which is spelled Q-u-i-s-t."

"The action was out there but it seems to be here, now," Quist said.

"So I'm taking the first plane I can get," Garvey said. "Somebody's got to cover you from the rear, buster. Our champagne kid isn't fooling."

Johnny Sands' face was drained of all its color. It looked sunken and old.

"Mike Marshall! It's hard to believe," he said.

"Believe it," Quist said.

They were in Johnny's suite at the Beaumont. Eddie was at the bar rustling drinks. Point by point Quist went over Garvey's report. Johnny listened, the corner of his mouth twitching. He tossed off the drink Eddie brought and handed back the empty glass for an instant refill.

"I dated that chick in Liebman's office a couple of times," Eddie said. "Thank God I did, or you might be thinking I—"

"Don't be crazy, Eddie," Johnny said, sounding almost angry. He looked at Quist, his eyes haggard. "If you didn't know me, Julian, and you heard all these facts, wouldn't you wonder if I wasn't trying to wipe out everyone who had the Trent thing on me?"

"I might," Quist said.

57

"This guy, whoever he is, knows everything," Eddie said. "How did he know you were going to stop off in Chicago, boss? Only you and me and the passenger agent at the airport knew that."

"This is the same guy who knew about the note we thought nobody knew about," Johnny said. "Now this frame-up is almost too good."

"Let's not make mysteries where we don't have to," Quist said. "Somebody didn't leave your party that night, or was in your house without having been to the party. Knowing you, anybody could have walked in off the street. A friend of Beverly Trent's who bled you, and now that there's no more blood, he's getting revenge. No mystery. The man was there—a member of the party or a stranger looking for Beverly. As for knowing you were stopping off at Chicago, he could have been standing behind you in the line at the ticket window."

"Thing I don't get," Eddie said. "Those calls to Max and Louie were made Friday afternoon, Mr. Quist says. You didn't decide till we were at the Los Angeles airport that you might stop off to see Jan in Chicago. How could he know a day ahead of you knew it yourself, boss?"

Johnny pressed the tips of his fingers against his eyes. "That isn't quite the way it was, Eddie. I called Jan in Chicago on Thursday night to ask if she'd see me if I stopped over. I didn't tell you, Eddie, because I knew you'd try to mother-hen me out of it."

Eddie looked hurt.

"I put on an act for you at the airport so you'd think it was an on-the-spot idea." Johnny looked at Quist. "You think the phone in my Beverly Hills house could be bugged?"

"The man knew," Quist said.

Johnny looked at his watch. "You still planning to go to Marian Scheer's party, pal?"

58

"If you are," Quist said. "I don't like the idea of your running around alone till we know more than we do."

Johnny laughed. "Alone? I'm taking three babes with me."

"Safety in numbers," Eddie said.

Quist put down his glass and stood up. The character lines in his face were etched deeper than normal. His pale blue eyes, fixed on Johnny, were cold.

"I don't run a detective agency, Johnny," he said. "I don't have a staff of tough guys who can bodyguard you. You want an opinion from me?"

"Sure, pal. You're the one I trust. You know that." Johnny looked haggard.

"One of two things is happening, Johnny. Or maybe it's two stages of the same thing. Somebody is methodically wiping out everyone who had anything to do with that champagne night, the part that involved moving Beverly Trent's body from your house to her apartment; Sabol, Liebman, the cop who knew something about it. Face it, there's still Eddie and you."

"Jesus!" Eddie said.

"If it's just some maniac getting revenge for what happened to Beverly Trent—Louise Hauptmann—you can count on his keeping after you. Eddie will come first, I think."

"Why me?" Eddie's voice was a whisper. "I had nothing to do with that night. I was in Acapulco."

"You helped cover it up," Quist said, apparently without feeling or emotion. "You will come first, Eddie, because I think he may have a special plan for Johnny. Johnny is to pay for it all. He was in Hollywood Friday morning. He could have taken care of Marshall, the cop. It will appear that he maneuvered Sabol to Chicago and Liebman to New York. He was in the airport when Sabol was shot. He was driving a rented car in the vicinity of the place where Liebman was run down. The car has a dented fender. Count on it, whatever happens to you, Eddie, it will look as though Johnny might have done it. Then the whistle gets blown on Johnny, he's charged with murder; the Beverly Trent story becomes public property. There's motive—to silence everyone who knew what happened to Beverly; opportunity—he was everywhere there was violence at the right time. You were blackmailed, Johnny, and it ended your career. You don't know who the blackmailer is, but you know it has to be one of the people in the know—Saból, Liebman, the cop, Eddie. Neat package. And there's an extra twist of the knife for you, Johnny. Dying is tough. Dying unexpectedly and suddenly is not the worst. But slow death, with your pride, your reputation, all the secrets of your life dug out by a smart district attorney, waiting in Death Row—all the things you cherish smashed—that will be one hell of a way to die, chum."

Johnny's eyes were closed, his face twisted with pain—or was it fear? "Who can it be, Julian?" he muttered. "Who, in the name of God, can it be?"

Quist ignored the question. "There's one possibility of an out for you," he said. Johnny's eyes popped opened. "This character, who's as mad as the March hare, may give you a chance. He'll make it clear to you that he has you cold, and then you'll start paying again—great, huge chunks until you're wiped out. You'll know that if you refuse you'll get it right between the eyes—in court or on a street corner, whichever way the whim hits him."

"So why are you telling me this?" Johnny asked. "It's all guesswork."

"I'm telling you in the hope that I'm scaring the hell out of you, Johnny. Julian Quist Associates is not equipped to handle this. We've figured it out for you, but we can't protect you."

"So give advice," Johnny said.

"To start with I'd send Eddie on a nice long vacation to like Timbuktu. He stays there, wearing a false face, till this guy is nailed. Then you go to the cops and lay it on the line—the truth about Beverly Trent. You didn't kill her, you only moved her. It'll make a lovely scandal, but you'll be alive. Police, the FBI, will be hunting for your man. They'll protect you in the process. Sooner or later they'll find this guy—he has to have some connection with Beverly Trent or with her earlier life as Louise Hauptmann. Once he's found you can start to breathe again."

"And the frame-up—the way he's lined up the killings so they look like I did it?"

"You go to the cops before he does and they're not so apt to buy it."

"Let me think about it."

"In this ball game you can die thinking," Quist said.

Johnny sat very still. Eddie, moistening dry lips, was watching him. Finally he said:

"I'd like to talk it over with Eddie. I'll let you know at Marian Scheer's party."

"If you don't go to the cops, Johnny," Quist said, "count me out from here on in."

"Why are we going to this party?" Lydia asked. She was sipping a dry martini at the bar in Quist's apartment. She was wearing a very elegant evening pants-suit. She looked ravishing in any kind of clothes, Quist thought. He was pouring himself a martini out of the glass maker. He looked very handsome in his dark blue tropical worsted suit with a white turtle-necked sweater, Lydia thought. We are truly the "beautiful people," she thought.

"I promised him," Quist said. He raised his glass.

61

"Cheers."

"But if he won't go to the police?"

"We will bid him a polite good night and go somewhere else."

"Like back here?" she asked.

"You'd like that?"

She smiled at him. "Better than anything else," she said.

"Like back here," he said. He bent down and kissed her on the cheek. "You smell good."

"I aim to please, sir," she said.

"May I say that in that department you never miss the bull's-eye, doll." He glanced at his watch. "Dan should be getting in from the Coast soon. I've left word for him to crash the party. Knowing Dan, he'll know more now than he did this morning; or at least have some sensible theories."

Marian Scheer, it turned out, was an expert at party-giving. What Johnny had called her "palace" was brilliantly lit from cellar to garret. There were bushels of flowers, strategically placed. A couple of men in white jackets and two or three maids in black uniforms with frilly white aprons circulated with trays of hot and cold hors d'oeuvres. There were bars on each floor, tended by men in red jackets. Nothing one could dream of wanting was missing, including a special greeter for Quist and Lydia.

He was a dark, eager-looking young man wearing a very mod double-breasted green suit made of a material that looked like velvet.

"Miss Morton—Mr. Quist? I'm Douglas Headman. Marian asked me to keep an eye open for you." Both eyes were fixed appreciatively on Lydia. "She's waiting for you upstairs."

Headman looked vaguely familiar to Quist. Then he

remembered this young man had been with Marian in the manager's office at the Garden on Saturday night.

Headman led the way upstairs. The guests all looked, Lydia thought, as though they had modeled their clothes for *Vogue* or *Esquire*. Marian Scheer surrounded herself for the most part with young people. The oldest person there, Lydia thought, was Johnny Sands, and yet he was the center of attention. Sticking close to him were three beautiful girls—a blonde, a brunette, and a redhead. They could have been hired from a model agency. Johnny, looking radiant and happy, attempted to introduce his ladies to Quist and Lydia.

"This is Dolores, and this is Betsy, and this is Claudine," he said, somehow managing to get his arms around all three of them.

"I'm Betsy," the redhead corrected him. She is Claudine." She indicated the blonde.

"I'm Dolores," the blonde said. "She is Claudine." She indicated the brunette.

"Names, names, names," Johnny laughed. "I concern myself only with measurements."

"Have you been thinking?" Quist asked.

"Oh, sure, pal," Johnny said. "First thing in the morning I follow your advice. Eddie didn't come because he's packing for his holiday. He decided on Venice. He says he always wanted to ride in a gondola. Now get yourselves drinks and try to catch up."

Marian Scheer worked her way through the crowd to say hello. Figuratively, Quist tipped his hat to her. She looked marvelous for whatever her age was. In fact you didn't think of age when you looked at her. She gave the impression of being just the right age for whatever world she chose to move in. Quist knew that on the way home Lydia would tell who had designed the fabulous evening gown Marian was wearing. Informal, she had said. The

63

dress could only be called informal because it revealed just a little too much—but excitingly—of all the good things about her figure.

"I see Douglas found you. It's delightful of you to come," she said.

"It was very nice of you to ask me," Lydia said.

Marian glanced at Quist and then smiled at Lydia. "I think so too," she said. "Understand, my dear, I only mean that if you weren't here Julian might find himself in danger. Don't worry, however. I never compete in a race in which I know I must come in second. Do let Douglas get you drinks. The buffet will be opened very presently, and Johnny has promised to do his thing for us later in the evening."

There were a handful of people there whom Quist and Lydia knew—a young actor Quist had helped launch on Broadway, a famous lady in the Women's Lib movement who had run a quite serious campaign, with Quist's help, to get the Democratic nomination for the President of the United States—"We died in New Hampshire, darlings, but we got ourselves heard from coast to coast"—Jud Walker, the official greeter for the City of New York, suave with old-world charm, one or two others. Marian had friends in all walks, and her party was, unexpectedly as far as Quist was concerned, quite fun. No one appeared to be bored. No one seemed self-conscious or tense, not even Johnny, who had a right to be tense. Most particularly not Johnny, who was literally surrounded by admirers in addition to his three dolls.

Quist and Lydia were talking to Jud Walker about Saturday night's benefit and the magic Johnny could work with an audience when someone struck a chord on the piano at the far end of the room. Johnny was standing on a chair, and his accompanist, Don Edwards, had appeared from somewhere. The room was instantly silent and Johnny began.

"*Miss Otis regrets she cannot have dinner tonight, Madam—*"

"There are only three people in the world who can sing those lyrics," Jud Walker said. "Noel Coward in his own way, Fred Astaire, and Johnny."

He sang it through. The applause was thunderous. Johnny raised his hands for silence. "So Miss Otis ain't here," he said, "but the dinner is. Follow me, pals!" He picked up his horn, which just happened to have appeared on the piano. *Miss Otis* became a stomping jazz rhythm as Johnny danced toward the dining room, his golden trumpet pointing to the sky.

Lydia found Douglas Headman's hand on her arm, guiding her. For just a moment the buffet table was a thing of beauty before the guests attacked it. A man in a chef's hat carved perfect roast beef, gorgeous hams, a monstrous turkey. There were hot silver chafing dishes, cold salads, a cold salmon as big as a small whale, cheeses, every imaginable kind of olives, relishes, and sauces. The little men in white coats circulated with a really great Burgundy.

"I wonder if Delbert Scheer knew how his money would be spent after he was gone," Quist said.

"I hope he doesn't mind," Lydia said. "I don't think I've ever seen anything like it. Please ignore me, darling. I'm going to make a pig of myself."

"Well stay ambulatory," Quist said. "Your Mr. Headman is on the make."

Out of the corner of his eye Quist saw Johnny heaping plates for his three dolls. Typically, Johnny himself was eating very little. He never ate before a performance. He could drink himself blind but not eat. And he was going to give a performance.

It was something when it happened. The guests, overstuffed and happy, draped themselves on every piece of furniture, sat on the floor, and Johnny began. Cole Porter and Gershwin were his boys that night. He sang one great song after another, adjusting to the size of the room so that it was all charmingly intimate. This was not the time or place for the horn. He would have to choose his own stopping time, Quist thought. No one here was going to budge until Johnny turned himself off.

Someone touched Quist's arm and he turned. It was Marian Scheer. Something had cracked the lacquered perfection of her face. She looked distressed.

"Can I speak to you a moment, Julian?"

She led him away from the guests and out into the little hall by the ancient elevator.

"There's a policeman downstairs asking for Johnny," she said. "Could you see what it is? If Johnny's stopped now my party is over."

"He's probably double-parked," Quist said.

Quist looked for Lydia and saw that Douglas Headman had moved in. He took the elevator down to the reception room. One look at the waiting man and Quist felt a cold finger move along his spine. He'd had dealings with this policeman once before. He was Lieutenant Kreevich of Homicide, a short square man trying to make his baby face look tough.

"Hullo, Quist," he said. "Matter of fact you're how I happen to be here."

"Oh?"

"Knew you were connected with Johnny Sands in a professional way. Had to locate him. Got one of your people on the phone—man named Garvey—and he told me there was a party here."

"You're not here to ask Johnny to sing for the Patrolmen's Benefit Ball," Quist said.

"No, I'm not. I'm sorry, but I'm going to have to interrupt him." Kreevich's head was raised, listening to Johnny's voice filtering down from the floor above.

"Is it a secret why?" Quist asked.

"Won't be a secret very shortly. Sands has a friend staying with him at the Beaumont."

Quist's mouth felt dry. "Eddie Wismer," he said.

"Yeah," Kreevich said. "Maid went into Sands' suite to turn down the beds. Somebody'd clobbered this Wismer guy. Head smashed in like an eggshell. He's a very, very dead man, Quist, and he didn't do it to himself."

"I imagine not," Quist said, his voice colorless. He had seen it coming, he told himself, and he hadn't made it urgent enough.

Kreevich was interested. "You knew this Wismer?"

"Well. And liked him. And I knew he was in danger but I couldn't convince him."

"Looks like I need to talk to you too," Kreevich said. "Will you get Johnny Sands for me?"

PART TWO

Chapter 1

MARIAN SCHEER WAS WAITING at the top of the stairs when Quist got there.

"I'm going to have to take Johnny away," he said.

"My party!" she said.

"It's serious, Marian. He won't be coming back. His friend Eddie Wismer—he's been killed."

"Oh God!"

"Try to keep things going for a while. I don't want the word spread until Johnny's out of here. I don't think he could face a crowd reaction."

"Of course."

Quist, looking for Lydia, spotted her across the room. She was seated in a high-backed armchair with young Mr. Headman, figuratively, surrounding her. He joined them.

"May I speak to you for a minute, doll," he said.

"I'll get you a drink," Headman said, and politely left them.

Quist let his hand rest gently on Lydia's shoulder. "It's Eddie," he said. "Somebody's killed him in Johnny's suite at the Beaumont.

Lydia's body stiffened. She looked up at Quist, her eyes wide, her lips parted.

71

"I've got to break it to Johnny and then go with him," Quist said. "I'm afraid you'll have to find your way home without me."

Lydia's eyes turned toward Douglas Headman who was on his way back from the bar with a drink. "I imagine I'll be offered help," she said. "How, Julian? Who?"

Quist shrugged. "Beaten to death. Who knows who? Fortunately for us our old friend Kreevich is in charge. He's waiting for Johnny downstairs."

"Anything I can do?"

"I don't think so. Except take care of yourself, love. There's something scary in the air."

"I'll be where you can reach me," she said. "My place or yours?"

"Better make it yours," Quist said. "God knows when I'll get home or who will be with me." He gave her shoulder a little squeeze and edged his way through the crowd to the piano. Johnny was in the middle of a rollicking chorus of "California, Here I Come." Quist leaned over Don Edwards', the accompanist's shoulder. "Cut it off, Don," he said. "I've got to take Johnny away for a bit. When he's gone keep the music going for a while."

"What's wrong?" Edwards asked.

"Eddie Wismer's been hurt," Quist said. "Johnny'll have to go to him."

"Hurt bad?" Edwards asked, not missing a beat on the piano.

"Bad," Quist said. The chorus came to an end and the party cheered and shouted out requests for other old favorites. Quist put his arm through Johnny's. "Got to talk to you for a moment, chum," he said.

Johnny's face was flushed with pleasure at what he was doing. "Later, pal," he said. "I'm just getting oiled up."

"Now," Quist said. Something in the hard set of his face, in his pale blue eyes, convinced Johnny that it was important. He raised his arms for silence.

"Freshen up, pals," he said. "I'll be back in a flash with a splash." He followed Quist out into the hall. "Your timing is lousy, Julian. I was just getting 'em real well hooked."

"Eddie's dead," Quist said.

Johnny froze. The color receded from his face. *"Eddie?"*

"He was beaten to death back in your suite at the Beaumont. The police are here for you. Questions."

Johnny bent over, almost double, hugging himself as if he'd been hit a punishing blow in the stomach. A little wailing cry escaped him, a cry of pain, that only Quist could hear over the rumble of voices in the room beyond. Don Edwards was playing a sad little interlude on the piano.

Johnny reached out and his hand closed on Quist's arm. The grip was painfully strong. He straightened up. His mouth was slack. He shook his head slowly from side to side, a movement that suggested stubborn disbelief.

"The maid who went in to turn down the beds found him," Quist said. "That's all I know. The man in charge is downstairs, waiting for you. Lieutenant Kreevich, and you're in luck. I've had dealings with him before and he's a decent guy."

"Give me a second," Johnny said in a choked voice. He let go of Quist's arm, straightened up, made a subconscious gesture with one hand to smooth down his hair. "That little jerk was the best friend I ever had. God forgive me, you were right, Julian. I should have gone to the cops yesterday."

"You should. Kreevich is waiting."

Kreevich had a police car waiting. He offered no resistance to the idea that Quist should go back to the Beaumont with them. He didn't say anything beyond the simple politeness of responding to an introduction until they were in the car.

"I know this is a blow to you, Mr. Sands," he said.

"Blow! Eddie was my best friend. He was fine when I left him—only a few hours ago."

"Just when was that?"

"About six-thirty," Johnny said. "I had three dolls to pick up on the way to the party. Eddie didn't come because he was going to Europe tomorrow. I left him packing."

"That checks," Kreevich said. "His half-packed suitcase is in the bedroom. Why was he going to Europe? Business?"

"Oh, God, Lieutenant, it's such a long story!"

"Mr. Quist implied that you knew Wismer was in some kind of danger. What kind? From whom?"

Johnny looked helplessly at Quist.

"It is a long story, Lieutenant," Quist said. "But this is the fourth friend of Johnny's to be murdered in the last forty-eight hours."

Kreevich's eyebrows shot up. "You're kidding!"

"One in California, one in Chicago, and two, now, here in New York."

"What other one here?" Kreevich asked.

"Hit-and-run on Madison Avenue early Sunday morning. A lawyer from California named Max Liebman."

Kreevich frowned. "There was nothing about that hit-and-run to suggest a deliberate homicide. Man was crossing the street and some drunk or hophead ran him down."

"I think you may change your mind," Quist said. The police car had pulled up outside the Beaumont. "I'll tell you about it when we get settled somewhere inside."

"I'd like to hear it now," Kreevich said, not moving to get out of the car.

"You, Johnny," Quist said.

"The whole thing?" Johnny asked.

"The whole thing; from the very beginning," Quist said.

And so Johnny told it, starting with the champagne party and Beverly Trent, and going on to the blackmailer, his retirement, and then the horror trail of the last hours—Louie Sabol in Chicago, Max Liebman, the word Dan Garvey had sent in on Marshall, the Hollywood cop."

"And you helped him cover all this, Quist?" Kreevich asked.

"I heard it all for the first time early Sunday morning," Quist said. "I urged Johnny to go to the police, but he resisted because of what it would do to him professionally. I did offer to get some facts for him, and I sent Dan Garvey out to Hollywood on Sunday afternoon. What Dan dug up—the fake messages from Johnny that sent Sabol to Chicago and Liebman to New York, the discovery that Marshall was dead, which we hadn't known when we started—persuaded me that I couldn't help Johnny any further unless he went to the police. I thought I saw some kind of a pattern; killing off all the people who knew the truth about the champagne party, leaving Johnny to the end. If I was right Eddie would be next. Late this afternoon I suggested that Eddie get out of town for a while, and I told Johnny I was through unless he went to the police. He promised me, earlier this evening, that he'd go to the police the first thing tomorrow morning."

"The District Attorney may take a dim view of your holding back vital information," Kreevich said.

"I wasn't aware how vital it was until late today," Quist said. "Johnny had the right to tell his own story. I kept pushing him."

"Screw the District Attorney!" Johnny exploded. "Somebody killed Eddie. That's your job, isn't it, Kreevich? All I care about is you get the sonofabitch who did it."

Kreevich opened the car door. "Let's go upstairs," he said.

Johnny didn't move. "Do I have to look at him?" he asked.

"Not now. The Medical Examiner has the body. Later you'll have to make a legal identification."

"Oh God!"

There had been a violence of some proportions in Suite 14B at the Beaumont. Two of the heavy comfortable leather chairs had been overturned. An embroidered runner on the table in the center of the room had been pulled off, taking a lamp and a couple of ashtrays with it. No one had slipped up behind Eddie Wismer and slugged him. Eddie had put up some kind of a fight, or at least had tried desperately to get away from his attacker.

There was a dark stain on the oriental rug that Quist guessed must have been made by Eddie's blood. A rough outline in chalk indicated where the body had been found.

There were two men in the room when Kreevich brought in Quist and Johnny. One was a hard-faced detective named Quillan; the other was a wiry, dark man with very bright black eyes who was the Beaumont's security officer. His name was Dodd.

Quillan reported. "Nothing much in the fingerprint department, Lieutenant. We raised quite a few. The deceased's, of course; some I think we'll find are Mr. Sands'. They're on his shaving things, and scattered around the place. Two or three other unidentified sets on glasses on the bar. People other than the deceased and Mr. Sands had drinks here."

"I for one, late in the afternoon," Quist said.

"The maid usually collects those used glasses when she comes in to turn down the beds, replaces them with fresh ones," Dodd said. "She didn't tonight, because the first thing she saw when she walked in here was the body. She high-tailed it out of here and sent for me."

"Nothing on the weapon," Quillan said. "It was wiped clean, or the killer wore gloves. The Lab will probably answer that for us."

"What was the weapon?" Quist asked.

"Silver candlestick," Quillan said. He gestured. "Mate to that one on the mantelpiece."

"Odd," Quist said, frowning.

"What's odd about it?" Kreevich asked. "You could kill a horse with it. Heavy, solid base."

"It suggests the murderer didn't come here prepared," Quist said, "or he changed his mind about what to use when he got here. How could he be sure he'd find a usable weapon here, if he planned to kill Eddie?"

"You suggesting someone came here, got in a quarrel with Wismer, picked up that candlestick in a rage and used it to kill?" Kreevich asked.

"Could be," Quist said, frowning. "But that wouldn't fit my pattern, Lieutenant. If the killer is the same man who did away with Marshall and Sabol and Liebman, he'd have come here prepared. He wouldn't have risked finding something here he could use."

"Unless he'd been here before," Dodd said, "and knew what he'd find." His bright black eyes shifted to Johnny.

Johnny had not advanced beyond the door of the room. He stood just to the right of it, leaning against the paneled wall. He seemed to be involved in a struggle to keep from looking at the stain and the chalked outline on the rug. He appeared to have some trouble breathing.

"You checked in here Saturday night, Mr. Sands?" Kreevich asked.

Johnny nodded.

"Correction," Dodd said. "The suite was reserved for him a couple of weeks ago and he was expected to sign in early Saturday evening. He didn't actually sign in until a quarter to four on Sunday morning."

"Saturday night—Sunday morning, all one piece of time," Johnny said. "You know about my flight in from Chicago, Lieutenant. I was way late. Actually Quist arranged a police escort for me from Kennedy. I went straight to the Garden, changed my clothes there, did my thing. I didn't check in here until it was all over." He shuddered. "That would have been just about the time Max Liebman was run over on the street."

"You've had these rooms for two days," Kreevich said. "I suppose there've been a lot of people in and out; friends, business contacts." He hesitated. "Women?"

Johnny's laugh was short and bitter. "My reputation precedes me," he said. "As a matter of fact, no women. No callers that I can think of except Julian this afternoon. But there could have been, I suppose."

"There were or there weren't," Kreevich said.

"Come on, Lieutenant, don't press," Johnny said. "I checked in here going on four o'clock on Sunday morning. While I was undressing to hit the sack I turned on the radio and heard about Max Liebman. I tried to call Julian but he didn't answer his phone." He turned his head to give Julian a sly look. "So I went to his apartment. That was about six in the morning. I spent almost all day Sunday there with him. Right, Julian?"

"Right."

"I hadn't had any sleep, except on the plane, since Friday night. I was pooped. I came back here from Julian's and damn near slept around the clock. Monday noon—

well, Monday noon I went to see a lady I know. I can produce her if I have to."

"Nobody's asking you for an alibi, Mr. Sands," Kreevich said. "We're asking who might have been here in the suite beside you and Wismer—and Mr. Quist."

"I got back here just before midnight on Monday. The lady's husband was due back." Johnny grinned. "I slept until fairly late this morning. Then I went to Julian's office to see him. Waited God knows how long for him to show up—half a bottle of Irish whiskey and a nap. Came back here, made some dates for the party on the phone. Then Julian came—my first visitor. Went to pick up my dates and on to the party."

"You said there could have been visitors?"

"Sure. Eddie was here, God bless him, all the times I was out. There could have been someone came in to see him or me."

"Wouldn't he have mentioned it?"

Johnny glanced at Quist. "He didn't mention anyone."

"I can tell you someone who was here," Quist said. "One of my associates, Miss Lydia Morton, came here to see Eddie while Johnny was in my office today."

"That explains the cigarettes with lipstick on 'em," Quillan said. "We knew there had been a woman here."

Kreevich made an impatient gesture. "Let's forget about your theory the killer is someone stalking everyone involved in the Beverly Trent business for a moment. Wismer have enemies—personal enemies?"

"Eddie? God, Lieutenant, everybody loved the little guy."

"Somebody didn't."

"It could be totally unrelated," Quist said. "A rather grim coincidence, but unrelated." He was frowning as he glanced at Dodd. "A hotel thief. He knows Johnny Sands is staying in the hotel. Johnny could be expected to have cash, probably some expensive jewelry. He lets himself into the room, and—"

"How does he let himself into the room?" Kreevich asked.

Dodd, the security man, shrugged. "There are five billion keys around a place like this. People are careless with them. It's not impossible for a key to get into the wrong hands—long enough to have a duplicate made. A maid comes in to make the beds, goes down the hall to get fresh linen, fixes the catch on the door so she can get back in without her key. They're trained not to do that, but it happens. She forgets to fix the catch. Anyone can walk in. We have the most foolproof locks money can buy, but a real pro—" Dodd shrugged. "The locks are only almost foolproof."

"So the thief gets into the room," Quist said. "Eddie is in the bedroom packing, hears something, surprises the thief and finds himself fighting for his life. The thief grabs the nearest thing at hand—the candlestick—and crushes Eddie's skull with it."

"Why didn't anybody hear anything? Why didn't Wismer yell for help?"

"These rooms are soundproofed," Dodd said. "He could yell his heart out and nobody would hear him."

Kreevich's eyes were narrowed, cold. "That's what you think happened, Quist?"

"No," Quist said, "but it could have been that way." He glanced at Dodd. "Nobody saw anyone come or go? Phone calls to the room—someone in the lobby?"

Dodd looked exasperated. "We weren't guarding Mr. Sands," he said. "We were aware that kids, fans, might try to get to him. Autographs. A chance to look at Johnny Sands, touch him, tear a button off his clothes for a keepsake. We were on the lookout in the lobby for some kind of action like that. The housekeeper on this floor had orders to keep an eye out for anyone loitering outside Fourteen B. But we weren't providing any special protection. Mr. Chambrun sees to it that special guests are not subjected to the annoyances that their particular reputation may attract."

"Who is Mr. Chambrun?" Kreevich asked.

Dodd appeared not to believe his ears. "My boss. The manager. What I'm saying is, when we have a famous politician or diplomat as guest, we look out for crackpots, pickets, someone who might be really dangerous. In Mr. Sands' case we were on the lookout for female idolaters."

"Do I have to stay here, Lieutenant?" Johnny asked. "I need a drink and I need it badly. And I don't want it in this room. I don't want to be here a moment longer than I have to."

"We've arranged to have your things moved to another room, Mr. Sands," Dodd said. "A valet is waiting to pack for you when you say the word."

"So can I go?" Johnny asked.

"I'm going to need a full and detailed statement from you," Kreevich said. "If you want to get yourself moved, I'll turn up with a police stenographer in about half an hour."

"I was dreaming I could stay at your place, Julian," Johnny said.

"Tonight I need to go over the whole thing with you, step by step," Kreevich said.

"Let me know when they turn you loose, chum," Quist said.

Quist found himself out in the hallway with Dodd, the security man. The valet had arrived and was helping Johnny pack.

"What's all this about some theory, some pattern?" Dodd asked.

"Long story," Quist said. "My problem is I thought Eddie was in danger, but I didn't make it urgent enough to him—or, I guess, to myself. A chain of killings in the last forty-eight hours. I thought Eddie might be next. Unfortunately I was right."

"And is there a next after that?"

"Could be."

"Sands, obviously."

"It could be Johnny's next and last on the list."

"Kreevich knows?"

"Yes."

"That takes some of the responsibility off my back," Dodd said. "But if there's any more violence in this hotel Mr. Chambrun will slice me into very small, very unedible pieces."

"I've heard about your Mr. Chambrun. Something of a legend in the hotel business."

"He asks, politely, will you stop in for a chat with him on your way out," Dodd said.

"How does he know I'm here?"

"He said you'd be coming with Johnny Sands."

"How did he know?"

"Around here we take it for granted he can see through brick walls," Dodd said. "Can I take you to him?"

"Why not? I've wanted to meet him."

It was something of an oddity that Quist had never met Pierre Chambrun. Dozens of his clients had stayed here at the Beaumont. He had been in and out a hundred times, dined here with Lydia, had cocktails in the Trapeze Bar, but to the best of his knowledge he had never laid eyes on the managing genius of the world's top luxury hotel.

Chambrun's office on the second floor was not like an office at all. It was a large room, beautifully furnished in a Renaissance style. There was nothing to suggest office except the four telephones on the beautifully carved Florentine desk. It was like a gracious living room. There was a sideboard in the far corner of the room on which rested an ornate Turkish coffee-making machine. There were beautiful cocktail, highball, and old-fashioned glasses and a staggering assortment of liquors and liqueurs. The first thing that caught Quist's eye was a marvelous blue-period Picasso on the wall opposite the desk. Then the man behind the desk took all his attention. Dodd introduced him to Pierre Chambrun.

Chambrun was a short, square, dark little man with black eyes buried in deep pouches. The eyes were so sharp that Quist thought they must be reading the maker's name on the inside of his shirt collar.

"Great pleasure to meet you at last, Mr. Quist," Chambrun said. Quist knew he was French but there was no trace of accent to his speech.

"My pleasure," Quist said.

"Will you help yourself to a drink or join me in some Turkish coffee? I warn you you must have a taste for it or you may find it a little overpowering. I like it very strong."

"I'll pour myself a brandy, if I may."

"There are several choices," Chambrun said. The deep-set eyes watched Quist go to the sideboard. "Italian," he said.

Quist turned. "I beg your pardon?"

"Italian. Your suit. Beautifully tailored, if I may say so."

"Thank you."

"Do sit down. This must have been a trying evening for you."

"Murder is not my favorite sport," Quist said. He sat down in a comfortable armchair opposite Chambrun. The hotel man was smoking a flat-shaped Egyptian cigarette.

"Curiosity can be an annoying habit," Chambrun said.

"Unfortunately it is overdeveloped in me. Running this hotel is like running a small city. We have our own shops, restaurants, bars, laundries, cleaning establishments, bank vaults, police force, a thousand and one details of a total life-operation. Only by staying curious can I be on top of everything. Violence is not unheard of here, just as it's not unheard of in the best-run city. But I take it as a personal affront."

"I can understand that."

"When the top public relations man in the city is indirectly involved I find myself concerned. A murder is bad publicity for the hotel. I have the feeling that this is not an ordinary murder, Mr. Quist; not a clumsy thief or someone who hated Edward Wismer."

"Oh?"

"Connections have not been made yet in the press, but I have made them," Chambrun said, his eyes now narrow slits. "A man named Max Liebman was a frequent guest of the hotel. He called me Saturday evening to find out when Johnny Sands was due to check in. He called me and not the desk because we were old friends. Later he died violently. Hours before that, it seems, a man named Louis Sabol was murdered in a Chicago airport. It turns out he was a friend of Johnny Sands'. Now, here in my hotel, another friend of Sands' is murdered. I smell connection, Mr. Quist."

Quist smiled faintly. "Your man Dodd says you can see through a brick wall."

"Then I'm right?"

"I think you're right. Johnny thinks you're right. We're trying to persuade the police that we're right."

"Is it illogical to assume that Johnny Sands may be next?"

"Not if there's any logic to any of it."

"Well," Chambrun said, his eyes glittering, "it won't

84

happen here in my hotel." He put out his cigarette, and his square fingers played with the lighter in front of him on the desk, turning it, twisting it. "My curiosity again. Something links these three dead men beyond their friendship with Johnny Sands; some event, something they did together in the past?"

Quist hesitated. The little man behind the desk was rather frighteningly clairvoyant. "You're right, of course, but I'm not at liberty to tell you what it is. It's Johnny's story—and now it also belongs to the police. But I will tell you something. There is a fourth man. He was a retired Los Angeles cop. He was found on Friday morning at the bottom of a cliff with his head smashed in like Eddie Wismer's—not the result of a fall."

Chambrun pursed his lips. "So the original thing, which you won't discuss, took place in Hollywood where they all lived." It wasn't a question. He lifted his heavy eyelids to stare at Quist. "Nothing we see these days is what it appears to be, Mr. Quist. We watch a prime minister or a president on television; he tells us his noble aims and plans; but behind it is his own conniving and maneuvering political activity. Behind a prim housewife's honest face is a lust for her neighbor's husband. Inside the strong man's body is a cancer eating away at his guts. The lavish tipper in my bar is a potential bankrupt. The truth is almost always invisible."

"An interesting but not too profound statement," Quist said. "What has it got to do with four murders, Mr. Chambrun?"

"I'll buy you the best dinner in town when you discover the truth behind what appears to be the truth." Chambrun smiles. "Without all the facts I'm just playing games. A magician attracts your attention with what appears to be the truth so that you won't see him adjust the false bottom in his top hat. Of course that false bottom is

85

the only truth. You will be a lot safer, Mr. Quist, while you hunt for a killer, if you keep that simple maxim in mind."

"I think I'm too pooped to think that through," Quist said. "But I'll remember that you warned me."

"Good man," Chambrun said. He stood up and held out his hand. "If I can be of any help to you, let me know. Be certain that nothing will happen to Johnny Sands in this hotel. I can't vouch for his safety anywhere else. Thanks for stopping by."

Quist smiled. "I think it's been a pleasure," he said.

Chapter 2

QUIST LET HIMSELF into his apartment. He hadn't been lying to Chambrun about being pooped. He also wished Chambrun hadn't started him wondering about false truths and magicians. It didn't make any sense, or did it?

He was tired, but he didn't feel like sleep. He loosened his tie and unbuttoned his shirt collar. He walked over to the bar and poured himself a brandy. Then he heard a sound and turned. Lydia was coming down the stairs from the second floor. She was still dressed as she had been at the party.

"I changed your mind," she said, in her husky voice. "I came here instead of going to my place as you suggested."

"My pleasure," Quist said. "Drink?"

"I'll make myself a scotch on the rocks," she said. "Are you expecting anyone?"

"Perhaps Johnny later," Quist said. "He's pretty well shaken up, doesn't want to stay at the Beaumont." He took one of his long, thin cigars from the box on the table and lit it.

"I wasn't playing the romantic theme by coming here, Julian," Lydia said, as she made herself a drink. "Young Mr. Douglas Headman was a little overpowering. He in-

87

sisted on seeing me home. There's no doorman at my place and I had a feeling he might be more than a little difficult. So I gave this address and said good night to him in the lobby, under the watchful eye of the doorman."

"Poor Headman," Quist said, grinning. "So much for youth's dreams. You do make people dream, darling."

"Can you tell me about Eddie, or are you too tired?"

He took a deep drag on his cigar. "Pretty shocking business," he said. "Somebody pulverized him with a silver candlestick. No known callers but you and me. You left lipstick on cigarette butts and fingerprints on your glass."

"How did the killer get into the suite?" Lydia asked.

"Maybe with a magic key, maybe Eddie let him in, unsuspecting."

"Poor little guy."

"Poor Eddie, poor Headman. The guys who make passes at you are to be pitied."

"Stop it, Julian. That's not funny. What's next?"

Quist shrugged. "Kreevich has the whole story, top to bottom. It's his party now. All we do is hold Johnny's hand if he asks. He's in shock, and I think he's scared."

"Wouldn't you be?" Lydia asked. "Some maniac wiping them out, one by one."

"I would. I am scared for him," Quist said. "What happened after we left the party?"

"People didn't realize he'd left for a while. Just thought he'd gone to answer the phone, or gone to the john, or something. Finally Mrs. Scheer told them that something had happened to a very close friend and Johnny'd gone to help." Lydia gave a rueful little laugh. "I was pretty well occupied trying to keep young Headman from raping me in public. As soon as Mrs. Scheer made her announcement people began to drift away, trying not to

88

seem too eager. Headman was blandly insisting that I say whether we go to his place or mine. I said mine, meaning here. Mrs. Scheer looked devastated, and Johnny's three dolls looked lost. I tried to persuade Headman that he owed it to Johnny to take care of them, that three gorgeous tootsies were an opportunity that he'd rarely have again."

"One thing about Mr. Headman, he has good taste," Quist said. "Did Dan show up?"

"No. I kept hoping he would, but he didn't."

"Funny," Quist said. "He's somewhere. That's how Kreevich knew we were at Marian Scheer's. He talked to Dan on the phone."

Dan Garvey was an impatient man. When he was on a job he wanted to wrap it up as quickly as possible. He hadn't beaten around a bush in years. When he wanted information he went straight to the horse's mouth to get it. He had a theory about the case; brother, father, ex-boy friend of Beverly Trent's was the blackmailer. The blackmailer was the killer. On his flying trip to Hollywood he had asked questions everywhere he went. Who knew Beverly Trent? Who were her friends? He came up with a name he knew, one Toby Tyler. Tyler had set out in life to be an actor, had gone to Hollywood for fame and fortune, had failed, and had turned to being a talent agent, trying to find jobs for people who were just as unlikely as he had been. A girl in Louis Sabol's office remembered that one of Tyler's clients had been Beverly Trent, a no-talent kid with extraordinary measurements. Toby Tyler was no longer in Hollywood. He had folded his tents a year or so ago and gone back to New York, where he was working as press agent for a chain of art movie houses. It was in that capacity that Garvey had met Tyler. Some film he was promoting had involved a client of Quist's, and Tyler had been in and out of the offices of Julian Quist Associates for a short spell.

When Garvey got back to New York from the Coast he found a message from Quist asking him to come to Marian Scheer's party. Garvey checked into the office to see if he could find an address for Toby Tyler. While he was looking for it there was a call from Lieutenant Kreevich asking where Johnny Sands could be located. Garvey told him the party. Kreevich didn't mention Eddie Wismer. Garvey told himself that at last Quist had made Johnny see the light and persuaded him to call the cops. He tried Toby Tyler on the phone they had for him, and by some miracle got him at home. Tyler would be delighted to meet him somewhere for a drink. Garvey suggested Willard's Backyard, a restaurant that served a marvelous steak. No reason why he shouldn't resolve the problem of hunger while he talked to Tyler. To hell with the party. It was more important to get on the trail of the long-lost brother, father, or ex-boy friend.

It cost him two steaks, but in the end Garvey decided it was worth it.

Toby Tyler may not have been a good actor, or a successful talent agent, but he was an extremely pleasant young man, attractive, not soured by failure. He was also hungry.

Garvey bought him a martini, ordered dinner, and asked his question. "I'm interested in a girl named Beverly Trent," he said.

"Long dead," Tyler said. "Poor old big-breasted Louise Hauptmann. That was her real name, you know. She finally couldn't make it, drank a gallon of liquor and consumed a bottle of downers—poof! End of a hopeless dream. You count that kind by the hundreds in Hollywood, even in the days when Hollywood was Hollywood."

"You remember anything about her?"

Tyler grinned. "How personal are you being?"

"I gather she slept around. I'm not asking about you."

"Johnny Sands was her big moment," Tyler said. His martini glass was empty. He looked questioningly at Garvey and Garvey signaled the waiter for a second round. "As a matter of fact she did herself in after a party at Johnny's. He'd had enough, and I guess she'd had one brush-off too many."

"It's generally known that she was at Johnny's champagne party?"

"I don't know how generally, but I know because I was there."

"At Johnny's party?"

"Yeah. I was at Chasen's when it started and I joined the crowd. I died fairly early in the proceedings. I don't have a head for champagne."

"Beverly came uninvited. Right?"

"Right. She arrived stoned. She had a couple of shots, and after screaming down the house she took off."

Garvey bit off his tongue to keep from saying that she hadn't taken off. "She came to the party alone?"

Tyler took a sip of his second martini. "It's my impression she had a guy with her, a bearded creep that I used to see around. I say it's my impression, because I didn't see them come together. But he was at the party for a while and I assumed it."

"He left with her?"

Tyler shook his head. "By that time, dad, I couldn't tell you who left with who. I was in the tank."

"You knew this beardo?"

"He was some kind of hippie freak," Tyler said. "He used to hang around places people went, mostly outside looking in. He had a tribe of grubby-looking girls who were always trailing him." Tyler shook his head. "You know, the first time I saw a picture of Charles Manson I thought it was the Chief."

"The Chief?"

"This guy had no name. People referred to him as the Chief. The Chief and his squaws. I think Beverly was part of his gang for a while. Or maybe she was just something on the side for him. Anyway, I saw her around with him from time to time." Tyler fished the olive out of his martini and ate it. "This Chief guy was bad news. The last I knew he'd disappeared from the Hollywood scene. One of his gals wandered into a big outdoor party being given by some big director type and set fire to herself."

"How's that?" Garvey was so startled he didn't look at the sizzling steak the waiter had put in front of him.

"Her clothes were soaked in gasoline," Tyler said. "She went up like a torch. The police went hunting for the Chief because they identified that particular slab of roast meat as one of his squaws. But the Chief had freaked out, split. So far as I know they never caught up with him."

Garvey looked down at his steak. "That story makes a great appetizer," he said. "However—" He attacked his steak. Tyler went after his own with enthusiasm. Burned-alive girls were forgotten for the moment. Finally Garvey tried again. "You did agenting for Beverly?"

Tyler nodded, his mouth full. Then he said: "God, these fried onions are good. What have I done to deserve all this, Dan?"

"You may have put me on the trail of a killer," Garvey said. "You read about Johnny Sands' pals—Sabol and Max Liebman?"

"Yeah. What's the connection with Beverly Trent?"

"I don't know. I'm trying to find out. You tried to sell her, you may know things you don't realize you know. Talk about her."

"She came to my office one day." Tyler made a wry

face. "My office, I may as well tell you, was over a very good kosher delicatessen. Nobody with diamonds came there, but I was in the yellow pages. So this chick walked in one day, and I took one look at her front, and I told myself I might be able to do business with the producer of the James Bond movies. That was a body! When she started to talk my heart sank. Boy, did she have speech problems. She sidled up to me and told me she was ready to do anything that was necessary to get her foot in the right door. I told her I only asked for ten percent, she should save the main course for some producer or director. But I took down her vital statistics and her name—Louise Hauptmann. I told her that would never do; remind people of the Lindbergh kidnapping. So we invented a name, then and there. Beverly, for Beverly Hills, Trent for my mother's favorite radio soap opera heroine, Helen Trent. I sent her some place they were auditioning show girls. She didn't come back for a couple of months. Somebody had taken one look at her equipment and glomed on. When she did come back she had some clothes and some cheap jewelry. So much for the first outing. I sent her somewhere else, and she was gone again for a couple of months. Next time she came back I told her I was a theatrical agent not a pimp. That ended our business association. I ran across her one day checking hats in a second-class night club. That's where Johnny Sands saw her. He was there to listen to some young singer he was promoting. So Beverly had her moment way up at the top. This time the clothes were outstanding, the jewelry very real. I suspect with her clothes on she was the biggest bore in the United States. So Johnny gave her the gate, from all accounts, and she died trying to scream her way back into his favor."

"It was after you stopped agenting her that she fell in with this Chief character?"

"Yeah. Look, friend, give me a minute to tackle this cow. It's so damned good I want to give it my undivided attention."

Garvey waited, impatient, sipping a good Burgundy while Tyler attacked his steak. Finally the young man leaned back with a sigh of pleasure.

"Ask me anything, dad. I'm in your debt forever."

"What else do you know about this Chief character? Know what his real name is?"

"Never heard him called anything but the Chief," Tyler said. "A weirdo of the first order. Black beard, black eyes, hair down below his shoulders. His eyes were crazy, kind of hot and burning."

"How did he eat?"

"With his fingers, I'd guess."

"I mean money. Where did he get the money to eat?"

"I suspect the squaws begged for him, whored for him, turned over anything they made at honest toil, as the saying goes. He had them mesmerized. I mean, you don't set fire to yourself at a party unless you're spooked. Like I tell you, when I first saw Manson's picture and heard all that jive about his girls and the Tate murders, I thought Manson was Chiefy boy. A closer look convinced me I was wrong—but out of the same mold."

"You've never seen him hanging around this man's town?"

"Lord, no. You think he's here?"

"I think he was on Saturday night and early Sunday morning," Garvey said.

Garvey didn't know about Eddie Wismer as he paid the check. If he had, he would have expanded his time span for the Chief's being in New York.

With Tyler on his way home, full of food and wine and happy, Garvey tried to reach Quist at the party. He was told by one of Marian Scheer's servants that Mr. Quist had left. He tried Quist's apartment without success. He kept trying at regular intervals until finally Quist answered.

"Where you been? I think I've got something for us," Garvey said.

"I've been attending a wake for Eddie Wismer," Quist said. "Somebody killed him."

They sat on Quist's terrace watching the moon go down—Quist, Lydia, and Garvey.

"It fits like a glove," Garvey said, his voice harsh. He was angry over what had happened to little Eddie Wismer; angry that he hadn't come up with facts sooner; angry that he didn't know where to put his hands on a murdering maniac.

"The Hollywood police could have something on this Chief character," Quist said. "According to your friend they were interested in him after the immolation at that party."

"It's a perfect fit," Garvey said. "This freak was at Johnny's party. Johnny should remember that. The Chief wasn't anyone you'd forget, according to Tyler. He came with Beverly, or he followed her there. He saw her go upstairs, followed her. Maybe he tried to spook her into getting some money from Johnny. That was his style. Waited around, expecting Johnny would eventually join her. Wandered around looking for something of value that wasn't nailed down. After a while he checks out on Beverly, finds her dead or dying—and sees the note! He gets out of there because he's connected to Beverly and he doesn't want the cops questioning him. Then, the next day, or the day after, he reads that Beverly has been found dead in her own apartment. It didn't take a genius to figure out what had happened."

Quist shook his head. "Just assuming that the Chief is

our boy, he didn't leave, Dan. He hung around some-where waiting to see what would happen. How else would he know that Sabol and Liebman were involved in moving Beverly's body?"

"So he hung around," Garvey said impatiently. "So he saw and he knew he had a meal ticket for the rest of his life. Johnny would pay forever rather than have it come out about Beverly. And Johnny did pay for two long years. So, when Johnny gets fed up and quits paying, quits his career, this freak has to figure a way to loosen him up again. He can wait a while. He's collected a small fortune. Johnny has clearly decided that he'd rather have the scandal break than go on being bled to death. So the freak bides his time until he reads that Johnny is going to New York to perform in a benefit. Then he sets out on his scheme to scare Johnny into paying; being a psycho he starts on a killing rampage."

Lydia shuddered. She reached out to Quist. Her hand was cold. "It's something out of a nightmare," she said.

Quist was silent, looking down at a little tugboat work-ing its way up the East River.

"You don't buy it?" Garvey asked, still angry.

"It could be," Quist said. "Johnny should remember if this Chief character was at his party. The Hollywood cops may have something on him. It fits so perfectly, Dan, that I find myself, for some reason, hesitating to buy it."

"What do you want, a written confession?"

"I don't know what I want, Dan. I tell myself there's a piece missing somewhere but I can't think what it is."

"Well, keep thinking, because for me it's airtight."

"The false bottom to the top hat," Quist said.

"You off your rocker?" Garvey asked. "What are you talking about?"

"I was warned tonight, by a very clever man, to watch

for the false bottom in the top hat," Quist said.

"I give up!" Garvey said. "You want me to lay this on the line for Kreevich?"

"Do that, Daniel. He'll get faster results from the Hollywood police than we can. I'll try to jog Johnny's memory about the party and whether he recalls this Chief character being there."

A call to Johnny's new room at the Beaumont got an answer from Sergeant Quillan, Kreevich's man. Johnny was still being questioned and dictating a statement for the Lieutenant. Quist asked to have him call when he was free.

"My friend Dan Garvey has something he thinks will interest the Lieutenant," Quist said.

"Will it wait?" Quillan asked.

"Perhaps it shouldn't," Quist said. He gestured to Dan, who came over and took the phone.

Quist went onto the terrace where Lydia still sat, huddled in a canvas deck chair. It was a warm night but she looked cold. Garvey's voice rumbled on in the room behind them.

"Get out of it, Julian," Lydia said. "Please!"

"I am out of it. It's Kreevich's ball game now."

"I know better. I know you. If Dan's right about this maniac all that you have to do is let your shadow fall across his path—"

"I'm the Invisible Man as far as Dan's maniac is concerned."

"No! It'll be all over the papers tomorrow. You're Johnny's P.R. man, his confidant, his friend. It's no secret. You're not invisible."

"So I'm visible. Why should this freak care about me? He wants Johnny to start paying again, or he wants to kill him because he's stopped paying. I don't matter to him."

"You will if you don't stop pushing, darling."

Quist looked at the red glow that was appearing in the East. "Johnny's my friend," he said.

"You're a fraud," Lydia said. "You pretend to be such a cynic about things, and you're just a sentimental slob."

"Would you back away if I was in Johnny's trouble?"

"That's different."

"In what way? You're my friend, aren't you?"

"You ape! I like to think—"

"You are, my darling, much more than just a friend. But in principle—"

It was daylight when Johnny called. He sounded exhausted.

"I take it you wanted to ask me about this Chief guy," he said. "Kreevich already asked me, thanks to Dan. I don't have an answer, pal. I heard about this guy and the doll who burned herself up at a party. If I ever saw him, I don't know it for certain."

"He wasn't at your party?"

"He might have been," Johnny said. "Christ, pal, everybody wears beards and long hair these days except us old creeps. There were half a dozen beards at my party. You know how it is, Julian. I've met thousands of people in my time who call me Johnny, like I was an old friend— people I never laid eyes on before. I don't know whether I know them or not. That night there was a crowd at Chasen's. I didn't count 'em. They all barged over to my place. Some of them I knew well, some I knew by sight. There may have been one or two I thought I knew, or ought to know, but didn't. Maybe this Chief guy was there. Maybe he came with Beverly and I thought he was there all the time. Maybe if I saw him I'd remember. But I just don't have an answer."

"Get some sleep," Quist said.

"Oh, God, how I need it." Johnny's voice broke. "You know, Julian, I can't believe it."

"Believe what?"

"That Eddie's gone. For twenty-five years he's been where I could call him if I needed him. I feel like I've lost an arm, you know what I mean?"

"I think I do. Get some sleep, Johnny."

"Maybe tomorrow I can come stay with you?"

"We'll talk about it. Call me."

"Yeah. Good night, pal."

At eleven o'clock the next morning, Wednesday, Lieutenant Kreevich turned up at Quist's office. He looked a hell of a lot brighter than Quist felt. He couldn't have had much more sleep.

"For what it's worth," he said, and dropped a long business envelope on Quist's desk.

It contained a report from the Hollywood police which they'd phoned to Kreevich. It turned out the Chief had the simple, unromantic name of David Harris.

"He had a few run-ins with the cops out there," Kreevich said, filling in. "He lived with a half a dozen gals and a couple of other guys in a kind of commune. They were picked up for loitering outside some Hollywood big shot's house. The same big shot whose party they spoiled later by having one of them burn herself alive. They were picked up on suspicion of drug using, but no conviction. Two of the girls served short terms for prostitution. The girl who burned herself up at the party was a runaway from a rich family somewhere in the Midwest. Her parents decided to bring an action against David Harris; morals violation involving a minor child. Harris beat the cops with a warrant by about an half an hour. He hasn't been seen or heard of since. Cops and the FBI still looking for him."

"I see he had a war record," Quist said, frowning at the paper.

"Two years in Vietnam. Commando group, decorated for bravery in action."

"Wouldn't be too upset by the sight of blood," Quist said.

"Wouldn't shrink from beating in a guy's head with a candlestick, either," Kreevich said.

Quist looked up. "You buy Dan's theory?"

"I got nothing else to buy at the moment," Kreevich said. "We'll try to locate him. He's the only suspect we can put a name to." The Lieutenant fumbled with a package of cigarettes and finally got one lit. "What do you suppose his next move will be?"

"On the surface," Quist said, "he would seem to be heading for one of two goals. He intends to kill everybody who had anything remotely to do with covering up the truth about Beverly Trent's death. That means Johnny is the last man alive and is his final target."

"Doesn't make sense," Kreevich said. "These men didn't kill the girl. They moved her body after she had killed herself."

"The man's a psycho. It doesn't have to make sense," Quist said. "The other possibility is that he may approach Johnny once more for money. 'You'll get what the others got if you don't pay up.'"

"Why did he wait so long if it's money he wants?" Kreevich asked. "Sands stopped paying two years ago when he retired."

"Two hundred thousand bucks carried him quite a long way," Quist said. "He could be hungry again. He knows it's no use threatening Johnny's career. Johnny's quit. So he will try to scare him into paying."

The buzzer on Quist's desk sounded and he picked up

the phone. Connie Parmalee informed him that Johnny Sands was on the line.

"Yes, Johnny?"

Johnny's voice was unrecognizable, cracked, high-pitched. "He's at it again, Julian."

"Who's at what, Johnny?"

"The blackmailer. The sonofabitch has put the bite on me again."

"Hold it, Johnny. Kreevich is here. I'll put you on the conference box." Quist leaned forward and threw a switch. "Speak of the devil," he said to Kreevich. Then: "You there, Johnny?"

"Of course I'm here. You gotta stop this, Lieutenant."

"How did he communicate?" Kreevich asked.

"Phone. Right here in my room at the Beaumont."

"Same voice you heard when it first started?"

"Sounded like it. I'm to pay up, or I'll get what the others got."

"How are you supposed to pay?" Kreevich asked.

"I'm to get the money," Johnny said. "A hundred grand. He'll let me how how to deliver it. If I don't—"

"Take it easy, Mr. Sands," Kreevich said. "We won't let him get to you."

"I'm coming over there," Johnny said. "I'm not going to stay five more minutes in this slaughterhouse. Send somebody to get me.

"There's a man outside your door, Mr. Sands. Call him in and let me talk to him," Kreevich said.

"I'm not opening this door to anyone but you, Lieutenant. How do I know who's really your man?"

Chapter 3

DAN GARVEY, LYDIA, and Connie Parmalee were gathered with Quist in his office. Kreevich had gone to the Beaumont to see Johnny.

"It's out of some crummy television drama," Garvey said, scowling.

"So were the Tate murders," Connie said, her amber-tinted granny glasses pushed up above her forehead. Her stenographer's notebook was tucked under one arm.

Quist sat at his desk, staring past his friends out the office window. The noise of a jet plane sifted through into the room.

"At least we know he's here in the city somewhere," Lydia said.

Quist turned his head, his pale blue eyes cold. "How do we know that?" he asked.

"The phone call. He's got to collect the money, doesn't he?"

"We don't know the phone call was local," Quist said. "We don't know where Johnny is supposed to deliver the money. Would you buy Mexico as an idea? That's the kind of place I'd choose to take delivery."

There was a moment of silence.

"Can the police really protect him?" Connie asked.

"It depends a good deal on what decision is made," Quist said. "If Johnny is going to pay, then our friend the Chief will set up some kind of delivery scheme that will make certain Johnny isn't covered by the police or anyone else. Out in the open no one can guarantee anything. If he isn't going to pay, he damn well better stay put somewhere, protected night and day, until we track down this maniac."

"Don't say 'we,' " Lydia said.

"Figure of speech."

"Lydia's right," Garvey said. "We know you like a book, Julian. When you say 'we' you mean we."

"Johnny's going to want to be with friends," Quist said. "Wouldn't you? He'd be as safe in my apartment as he would anywhere. I'm not going to turn my back on him, Dan, just because I might be in the line of fire."

"So you want to be a hero, be a hero!" Garvey said.

The buzzer sounded on Quist's desk and he switched on the squawk box. The voice of Miss Gloria Chard, the receptionist, came through. "There's a Mr. Headman out here to see Lydia," she said. She giggled. "He's most insistent."

"Oh God!" Lydia said. "He's called me three times this morning to ask me for lunch. He won't take no for an answer, apparently."

Quist smiled. "Gloria? Tell Mr. Headman Miss Morton is in conference and tied up indefinitely."

Gloria was struggling with laughter. "That being the case have you any objection to my substituting for Lydia at lunch?"

"Make sure it's expensive," Quist said, and turned off the box.

"A most determined young man," Lydia said.

"You don't mind Gloria's stealing him away from you?" Quist asked.

103

"I couldn't be more delighted," Lydia said, sounding almost prim.

"Dog in the manger," Quist said.

"Oh, cut it out, Julian."

Garvey made an impatient gesture. "So you're going to take Johnny under your wing, keep him at your place?"

"If he asks," Quist said.

"Oh, he'll ask," Garvey said. "You'd better hire a bartender for his visit."

Quist ignored the crack. The three people in his office were closer to him in their various ways than anyone else had ever been. Dan Garvey, blustering, dark-mooded, would go just as far out for him, Quist knew, as you could expect another human being to go. He would complain, and grouse, and argue, but he would go along with any decision Quist made. Quist had only to ask him and Garvey would face any danger, fight any battle. The result was that Quist, in turn, would go just as far for Garvey.

Lydia was not just a beautiful and super-desirable girl who shared his bed with him. Their mutual love for each other was so deep, so full of joy, provided such an incomparable companionship, that each of them was committed beyond anything a legal or religious tie could have provided. Quist had been playing the field when Lydia applied for a job at Julian Quist Associates. Women were attracted to him and he enjoyed love-making as a game. The first time they had come together Quist had thought of it as promising just another charming interlude. They were both swept off their feet by each other. From that moment on there was no one else for either of them. No questions asked about the past. They assured each other that they weren't bound; if Lydia saw another man she wanted she was free to go. He was equally free, Lydia assured him. But nobody went anywhere. Why not marry,

Garvey had asked Quist. It was quite simple. The relationship was so perfect as it was that neither one wanted to risk changing it in any way. Perhaps, some day, if they thought of children—

Connie Parmalee, Quist's secretary, was something else again. Quist was her life, as the boss often is for the girl who works close to him. She shared his business secrets, she knew all there was to know about him. She was sensitive to his moods, his needs, his appetites. And she knew that if she ever let down the bars and showed him how much she wanted him, how available she was, that their association would come to an end. So she lived her private life, had her secondary romances, and served the man she really loved with an efficiency that was beyond description. She had some kind of psychic tie to him that made it possible for her to anticipate his needs. More than once she had left a party, or a bed, because she suddenly knew that Quist needed her.

Quist was acutely aware of what these three people meant to him. He was prepared to go out on a limb for Johnny Sands. Johnny was his friend, he had said, but not a friend in a sense that these three people were. Was he endangering them by not pulling totally away from Johnny?

"I think," he said unexpectedly, "that this is a decision we should all make."

"What decision?" Garvey said.

"About Johnny. He's got big trouble. My impulse is to help him, to offer him shelter and what protection I can. But it will involve all of you, so you should have a say in it."

"We'll decide it democratically," Garvey said, his voice dripping acid. "We'll take a vote and it will be three to one against. So we'll do it because your one vote is the deciding one."

Connie adjusted her granny glasses on the bridge of her nose. "One of the reasons we go for you, boss, is because you're the kind of guy you are. Being the kind of guy you are you have to help Johnny Sands. So we have to go along, don't we?"

Quist looked at Lydia. Her answer was in her dark, violet eyes. He didn't need words.

"Thanks," Quist said.

"Don't thank me," Garvey said. "I'm a no-voter, but I have to go along. Democracy."

"Bless you, my children," Quist said.

And then Johnny Sands arrived with Kreevich and his Sergeant Quillan. Johnny was a shocking sight. He hadn't shaved, and the stubble on his cheeks and chin was unexpectedly gray. His seersucker suit looked as if he'd slept in it. His eyes were bloodshot and there were dark circles under them. He looked as if he was fighting a decision—to laugh or cry.

He dropped down in a chair by Quist's desk. Connie was suddenly beside him with a glass of Irish.

"Thanks, doll," Johnny said.

"How serious were you about putting Sands up in your apartment, Quist?" Lieutenant Kreevich asked.

"Serious."

"It would be better than a hotel," Kreevich said.

"And better than a jail in protective custody," Johnny said bitterly.

"Not so many people coming and going," Kreevich said. "We can keep a man round the clock either outside your front door or inside."

"For the rest of my life?" Johnny asked.

"If you're willing, Quist, I'll leave word at the Beaumont that Sands can be reached at your number," Kreevich said. "The blackmailer will obviously call again. All right to bug your phone? That way we may be able to trace an incoming call while they're talking."

"Whatever you want," Quist said.

Kreevich signaled to Quillan and the sergeant went out.

"Quillan will stay with Sands until I have a regular routine set up," Kreevich said. "Who has access to your apartment besides yourself, Quist?"

"The people you see here."

"Keys?"

"Yes."

Kreevich turned to Johnny, his face grim. "You've asked for protection, Sands, but I can only give it to you if you follow my instructions right down the line."

"Like what?" Johnny asked. The Irish had improved his color.

"We take you from here to Beekman Place and Quist's apartment. Once there you're not to step out of the place for anything. Not *anything!* You get a call from the black-mailer, we'll know. You stall him as long as you can in the hope we can trace the call."

"How do I get the money for him?" Johnny asked. "You don't find a hundred grand in a bushel basket on the street corner."

"One of us can arrange that for you," Quist said.

"You're going to be asked to deliver the money alone," Kreevich said. "No cops, no one following you. You don't move until we've worked out a plan. You understand?"

"Yeah."

Kreevich showed an understanding of his man that surprised and reassured Quist. "You're a free spirit, Sands," the Lieutenant said. "You're used to snapping your fingers and getting what you want. You're going to think of some gal you'd like to see, or some spot you'd like to go. You can't do either without a 'yes' from me. You're a voluntary prisoner, you understand?"

Johnny gave Kreevich the look of a sly child. "If Julian says I can have a girl in, you got objections, Lieutenant?"

"Nobody, unless I've checked them out, top to bottom. Nobody but the people in this room."

Johnny glanced at Lydia and then at Connie. "Well, if they're friendly who could ask for anything more?"

"Cut it out, Johnny," Quist said sharply.

"Just a gag, pal. Just a song title, as a matter of fact. 'Who Could Ask For Anything More?' "

"If it's all right with you, Quist, we'll wait here for a little," Kreevich said, "until we can get your phone fixed."

"Maybe we should get married, pal," Johnny said. "Looks like I'm going to be your Siamese twin." There was a suspicious glisten of tears in his eyes.

Quist made a little gesture which the others understood. They drifted out of the office leaving Quist alone with Johnny. The moment they were alone Johnny covered his face with his hands and was shaken by deep, wracking sobs.

Quist sat very still, not moving. Eventually Johnny fished a handkerchief out of his pocket and blew his nose hard.

"Goddam baby," he muttered.

"Have another slug of booze," Quist said.

Johnny got up, walked over to the sideboard, and poured. When he finally turned back he was reasonably in control.

"I wouldn't go through all this mumbo jumbo if it wasn't for Eddie," he said.

"How do you mean?"

"I'd take my chances," Johnny said. "Hit the high spots, live my life. He might get to me, he might not. But there's a chance he would—and get away with it! I'm not going to let him get away with it, pal. He's going to pay for what happened to Eddie."

"But you're going to pay?"

"Not goddam likely," Johnny said. "But I'm going to go through the motions of paying. I'll raise the cash, because he may be watching somehow. I'll go where he tells me to go with it, but Kreevich will cover me somehow. I have just one dream."

"Oh?"

"I dream that I get my hands on the sonofabitch before Kreevich does!" The corner of his mouth twitched. "Did I say 'thank you' for giving me shelter?"

"We'll play it cool," Quist said.

"How cool would you be if your best friend died for you?" Johnny said. "All because I had a yen for that stupid broad, Beverly Trent. You know something? She wasn't even any good!"

Quist and Johnny were taken to Beekman Place in a police car, with Kreevich riding on the front seat with the driver. A marked patrol car followed. Getting in the car at the office and out of it at the apartment Johnny was surrounded by uniformed and plainclothes cops. Only a sniper, prearranged and perfectly placed, would have had any chance of getting at him.

The apartment itself was sealed off from the outside world. One of Kreevich's men was placed in the lobby to bolster the regular attendant. Another was placed in the twentieth-floor hallway outside the front door of Quist's apartment. A third man was to be in the apartment and a fourth stationed at the rear where the service elevator was located and the fire stairs.

"Nobody's going to get near the front or back door unless they come shooting," Kreevich said, when he was satisfied. "I want you, Sands, and you, Quist, to be clear about one thing. You will not open the front or back door to anyone—not your friends with the keys—not anyone until the policeman on duty gives you an okay."

"You don't trust my people?" Quist asked, frowning.

"Sure I trust them," Kreevich said. "But I don't want the doors opened if there is any traffic outside in the hall. My men will wait till the hallways are clear of people before he gives you the okay to open the doors. Understood?"

Quist nodded. Johnny seemed to have lost interest. He had headed, with purpose, toward the bar.

"There is a man set up in the basement to monitor your phone," Kreevich went on. "If your phone rings, let it go three times. Pick it up on the fourth ring and my man will do the same. The point is to keep a caller from hearing an extra click."

"What is Johnny's tack to be if the blackmailer called?" Quist asked.

"Stall," Kreevich said. "Stall, stall, stall. We need to try to trace the call."

"He's to agree to instructions?"

"He's to agree. We'll figure out what to do after he gets them."

"And where will you be?" Quist asked.

"Call this number," Kreevich said, handing Quist a slip of paper. "They'll reach me within minutes, wherever I am."

"So that's it?"

"That's it." Kreevich looked at Johnny, who was pouring himself a drink. "Try to keep him from getting impatient. The call may come soon, or maybe it won't come for a day or two. I imagine soon. He'll want to move before we can get too well organized."

The blackmail money had been arranged for before they'd left Quist's office. It had turned out to be remarkably simple. Johnny's credit appeared to be unlimited. A call to his Los Angeles bank by Quist's bank in New York had set it up in a matter of minutes. Sergeant Quillan had gone to the bank and collected the cash in tens, twenties, and one hundreds. It had been packed in a pigskin bag that stood now in the hall closet just off the front door.

"If Johnny is asked to start somewhere at once with the money?"

"Call me, take ten minutes, and go," Kreevich said. "He'll be covered like a tent."

"Which will be strictly against orders," Quist said.

"I think we can promise to be pretty invisible," Kreevich said.

When Kreevich had gone Johnny turned from the bar, a half-empty glass in his hand.

"I never felt so helpless in my life," he said. "What the hell good is all this protection and this phone tapping? It only means nothing is going to happen here. This creep isn't so crazy as to walk into this kind of obvious trap. He'll tell me where to go with the bread, and wherever that is the fuzz won't be able to cover me." He swallowed the rest of his drink. "You got a gun, pal? A hand gun?"

"No. Why?"

"I told you a while back I wanted to live," Johnny said. The corner of his mouth twitched. "Right now I feel as if all I want is to come face to face with this bastard and kill him, cold, in his tracks." He turned away. "Eddie never had a chance, never knew what was coming. I'd like this jerk to know, for thirty seconds, that he'd struck out—and then let him have it."

"When Kreevich gets him he'll have longer than that to anticipate what's coming to him," Quist said.

"Kreevich-Smeevich," Johnny said. "He's a routine cop. This guy is too smart for him. Look how he set me up? I could have killed Marshall, the cop. I was in Hollywood last Friday morning. He set me up in Chicago so it looks as if I could have killed Louie Sabol. He got Max Liebman here, dented up my car, fingered me for that. He's too smart for a gumshoe type like Kreevich. He'll get me to some lonely spot with the money and maybe wipe me out after he's got it. I want a gun, Julian. Help me to get a gun so I have a chance."

The telephone rang.

The two men stared at each other. Quist gestured Johnny to the phone.

A second ring.

"Wait!" Quist said sharply.

The third ring. Johnny's hand was on the phone. He picked it up as the fourth ring started.

"Hello?" He looked at Quist and nodded his head vigorously. "Yes, you bastard, this is Johnny Sands . . . Yes, I've got it . . . Madison Square Garden! . . . Yes . . . Yes . . . I understand what you're saying, but I'm not sure that I want to risk . . ."

Slowly Johnny put down the phone, his hand shaking. "I couldn't stall him. The sonofabitch is out of his mind!"

Quist had the slip of paper with Kreevich's number on it. The Lieutenant, he thought, couldn't have gotten more than a block away. "Quickly, Johnny. What are you to do?"

Johnny shook his head from side to side. "Go to a hockey game tonight at Madison Square Garden," he said. "There's a ticket held for me at the box office. I take the money. I wait for someone to ask me for it. I go alone. If the cops stake out the joint the price will go up."

Quist was dialing Kreevich's number.

"It's screwy!" Johnny said. "How can he tell whether the place is staked out? There'll be fifteen thousand people there. What has he got, a radar system for spotting cops?"

Someone on the other end was trying to reach Kreevich on the car telephone. Presently the Lieutenant's voice came through.

"So soon?" he said. 'I'll be back there in ten minutes. Where's the delivery spot?"

"Madison Square Garden—at tonight's hockey game."

"You have to be kidding," Kreevich said.

Chapter 4

THERE WAS A TICKET reserved for Johnny Sands at the Garden. It was a very good seat, located at center ice.

Kreevich looked as if he couldn't believe it. He checked with his man monitoring Quist's phone in the basement. There'd been no time to check the source of the call, but the message had been taped. It was exactly as Johnny had reported it to be.

"It doesn't make the slightest sense," Kreevich said. He glanced at his watch. "We have four hours to set things up. We can have Sands literally surrounded; we can have every exist covered. If somebody takes the bag of money from Sands we can have him wrapped up before he's gone twenty yards. Nobody in his right mind would plan such a way to collect loot."

"Who says he's in his right mind?" Johnny asked. "The last three days ought to convince you. You know something?"

"What?" Kreevich asked.

"I'll bet he's figured out a way to make it work. Everything else has worked for him."

"Not a snowball's chance," Kreevich said, but he looked worried.

The stake-out was carefully and efficiently planned.

Johnny was to take his seat, carrying the pigskin bag with the money in it. Exits would be covered. There would be some twenty men spotted within easy distance of Johnny's seat. The Garden was a sellout, because the Rangers were playing their top rivals, the Boston Bruins, but Quist, through special pull he had, got four seats for himself, Lydia, Garvey and Connie Parmalee. They were located across the rink from Johnny, but they would have a full view of any action that took place. There was something macabre about going to the Garden, armed with a pair of opera glasses, to watch a murderer pick up a small fortune in cash and then be grabbed by the police. There simply was no way for him not to be grabbed.

Kreevich was prepared for almost anything. Criminals have a way of repeating their method of operation. This man had tried a false bomb scare to maneuver Johnny back to the Chicago airport on Saturday night. A false bomb scare might be his M.O. this time. This could empty Madison Square Garden of its customers, the two hockey clubs, the ushers and other personnel. It could create a panic situation. In the confusion the man they were after might expect to be able to grab the money bag from Johnny and get away with it. It wouldn't work because Kreevich's men would be ordered to hold their ground no matter what the confusion. There was no way for the killer to work it—and yet—and yet— Why set up an impossible situation unless there was a way?

"There is no such thing as an invisible man," Kreevich tried to reassure himself and the others. "He's got to try to walk away with that bag in his hand. And even if there is such a thing as an invisible man—"

Quist, listening, laughed.

"—even if there is, the bag isn't!" Kreevich finished.

Johnny made his plea again, this time to Kreevich, for a gun. "I've got a right to some protection," he said.

"Count on us," Kreevich said.

Quist had his own anxiety about the situation and he managed to maneuver Kreevich into his study so he could put it to him.

"You know Pierre Chambrun, the manager of the Beaumont?" Quist asked the Lieutenant.

"Met him," Kreevich said. "He's had some involvements with my department from time to time. Bright guy."

"He warned me about something last night," Quist said. "A magician always draws your attention to what you're supposed to think is the truth to keep you from noticing the false bottom in his top hat."

Kreevich was tired and irritated. "So what?" he said.

"You and I know there's no way this fellow can get away with that bag of money," Quist said. "It's just plain impossible. So isn't there a chance we're being led down the garden path—to keep us from seeing the false bottom in the top hat?"

"Would you mind coming to the point, Quist? I haven't time to—"

"He doesn't intend to go after the money. Has no interest in it," Quist said.

"A hundred grand?"

"He's embarked on a blood bath," Quist said. "Marshall, the Hollywood cop, Sabol, Liebman, Eddie Wismer. Johnny is the last of the people involved in the Beverly Trent business. He can't get to Johnny here. He can't get to him on the street, surrounded by cops. So he arranges for him to be at the Garden. He picks out an exact seat for him. Johnny becomes a perfect target. He doesn't have to be close to him. He could be in the top balcony with a high-powered rifle. No one will be watching. They'll be staring bug-eyed at the hockey game. He fires—Johnny keels over. Your men rush to Johnny to see what's happened and our boy walks away. He leaves his rifle behind, goes to the men's room, and suddenly you're confronted with the problem of picking him out of fifteen thousand people. And Johnny is dead, which is all he's after."

"You and your top hat!" Kreevich muttered.

"It's the only reason I can see for setting up a situation that won't work," Quist said. "He doesn't mean it to work."

Kreevich's cigarette glowed hot as he dragged on it. "Damn!" he said. "All right! Nobody can get close enough to Sands with a hand gun. We've got men all around him, watching for anything. Your rifleman is the only possibility. He'd have to be across the way to get a clear shot at Sands. We'll cover that area like a tent."

"Don't go through with it," Quist said.

"We've got a mass murderer inside the four walls of a building," Kreevich said. "I'm not going to lose that chance."

"Give Johnny a chance to back out," Quist said. "It's his life you're playing games with. He ought to have some say in the matter."

"I guess that's reasonable," Kreevich said.

Johnny was summoned into the study. He had a kind of glazed look. Quist laid out his theory. Johnny listened as though he wasn't quite hearing it.

"Quist has convinced me I ought to give you the chance to pull out," Kreevich said.

Johnny moistened his lips. "What are my chances—if Julian is right?"

"I think we can cover you," Kreevich said. "Ninety percent sure. Ten percent risk."

Johnny's grin was false. "You run a ten percent chance every day you'll break your neck in the bathtub," he said. "I like the odds."

"Don't be a sucker," Quist said, his voice harsh. "A man with a high-powered rifle, telescopic site, can get you right between the eyes with no trouble. The odds are nothing like nine to one."

"Get me and get away with it?" Johnny asked.

"It may not matter to him about getting away with it," Quist said. "You're the last one on his list, if we've guessed right about him."

"Thanks for worrying about me, pal," Johnny said. He drew a deep breath. "I want to get it over with. I'll take the chance, Lieutenant."

"You're an idiot," Quist said.

Johnny gave him a playful poke in the chest. "You'll have the best seats in the house to watch it, pal."

Madison Square Garden was jammed with people. Bright lights bore down on the clean surface of the ice with its blue and red zone stripes and its face-off circles. The Rangers and the Bruins were on the ice, taking casual shots at their goalies in the pregame warm-up. This was a crowd pleaser, with the Bruins showing the great Bobby Orr, Phil Esposito and company, and the Rangers with their high scoring line of Hadfield, Ratelle, and Gilbert. The goalies stood in their nets, masked, looking like something out of a horror movie.

The organ struck a chord and the crowd stood for the playing of "The Star-Spangled Banner." Then began a shrieking and yelling as the players who were not starting skated to their respective benches and the referee prepared to drop the puck for the opening face-off.

Across ice from the Rangers' bench Quist, Lydia, Dan Garvey and Connie Parmalee sat together. They weren't watching the game. Quist, opera glasses raised to his eyes, was staring across the ice at Johnny Sands. He had seen him come into the arena a few minutes ago, carrying the pigskin bag, being guided to his seat by a uniformed usher. It was slow going because he was recognized. People waved at him and shouted to him and Johnny waved back, smiling a sort of fixed smile. A few people crowded up to him to ask for autographs.

"He was a fool to come," Garvey muttered, at Quist's elbow. "It can all be over in a few seconds. They can't protect him in that crush."

But Johnny finally got to his seat. He sat down, the pigskin bag between his legs. Quist's glasses were so good he could see the little trickle of sweat running down Johnny's cheek. He saw Johnny's eyes sweep the seats across the rink. That was where the sniper would most probably be located—if there was a sniper.

"It takes a kind of crazy guts to sit there and make himself a target," Garvey said.

Bedlam broke loose in the Garden. The game was underway. Quist never once looked at what was happening on the ice. Two things could happen to Johnny, and either of them would probably take place while the excitement was greatest on the ice, while fifteen thousand people were riveted on the game. The sniper could take his shot at Johnny, or someone would approach him and ask for the pigskin bag. Quist knew that only a few seats from Johnny were some of Kreevich's men. A man asking for the bag would never get away with it. But the sniper—

Quist's muscles were so tensed as he waited that they ached. He was aware that Lydia's fingernails were biting into the flesh of his wrist. And thousands of people screamed with joy at the speed, and skill, and violence that was being exhibited on the ice.

The first twenty-minute period of play came to an end. Johnny had been like a statue across the way, the bag resting between his legs. Now, in the intermission, people crowded around him to speak to him, ask for autographs, to touch him as though that would somehow bring them luck or health.

Quist stood up. "I don't think I can take any more of this," he said. "I'm going to move around to the other side. I feel, somehow, that if I'm close to him it might help. Nothing's going to happen in the intermission. Too many people paying attention to Johnny."

"I'll go with you," Lydia said.

"Stay here," Quist said. "You'll be in the target area over there."

"And you?" she asked.

"Like they used to say in the army, if a bullet's got my name on it I can't duck it."

"Me either," Lydia said, and stood up, clinging closely to his arm.

They edged their way through the milling crowd around the far end of the rink toward Johnny's place in the crowd. At one entrance they encountered Kreevich.

"I feel ten years older," the Lieutenant said. "I almost wish I hadn't brought him here."

"Any kind of report at all to you?" Quist asked.

"I have men circulating the opposite side of the rink. We haven't spotted anyone carrying anything that might be a rifle—not even broken down."

"Not hard to hide under an overcoat," Quist said.

"Don't I know it."

There was no way to get close to Johnny without blocking someone's view of the game. There wasn't an empty seat in the house. Quist and Lydia stood by Kreevich in the entryway and waited as the game began again. The screaming and yelling was high-pitched again and Johnny had resumed his frozen position, bag between his legs, waiting—waiting—

It seemed a very long time before the second and then the third periods were over and the crowd began to move toward the exits on their way home.

"Who won?" Lydia asked in a small voice.

"I haven't the faintest," Quist said.

"Rangers, three–two," Kreevich said. He was watching Johnny, who hadn't made any move to leave his seat.

Quist felt an inner alarm tightening his gut muscles. Why was Johnny sitting there so still? Why hadn't he moved with the crowd? Obviously no one was going to ask him for the bag now. Had something happened to him? Quist started to move, when Johnny stood up, gripping the bag. Relief surged over Quist.

The crowd, as always, was thinning out fast. Johnny started along the aisle behind his seat toward the entry where Quist and Lydia and Kreevich waited. He looked old and tired, the bag seeming to weigh him down. A hundred thousand dollars in paper weighed more than a ham sandwich, Quist thought. Quist was reminded of Willy Loman, Arthur Miller's salesman, weighted down by his sample case.

Then there was a totally unexpected confrontation. Out of nowhere appeared a familiar figure. Douglas Headman, the young man who had been hounding Lydia, faced Johnny in the aisle, smiling. He said something to Johnny which they couldn't hear at that distance, and Johnny held out the pigskin bag to him. Headman took it and then, unbelievably, Johnny sprang at him, swinging punches wildly. Headman staggered back and Johnny was at him, trying to grab him by the throat. Headman reacted now, violently. He swung a vicious right cross to Johnny's jaw. He dropped the bag and pounded a left to Johnny's stomach and Johnny went down. Headman made no move to run or get away. He stood staring down at Johnny as though he couldn't believe what he saw.

And then he was surrounded by Kreevich's men, his arms grabbed and held. Quist and Kreevich reached him.

Johnny, a trickle of blood running out of the corner of his mouth, was struggling to his feet. Quist helped him.

"The sonofabitch asked for the bag," Johnny muttered. "He's the one."

Headman looked utterly bewildered. "What happened to him?" he asked, his voice shaken. "I offered to carry his bag for him and he jumped me. Look, Johnny, I hope I haven't hurt you, but when you jumped me I just reacted in self-defense. What's wrong? What have I done?"

"This whole thing is absolutely senseless," Headman said.

They were in the Captain's office of the local police precinct building—Headman, Kreevich, Johnny, half a dozen plainclothes detectives, Quist and Garvey. The pigskin bag was on the desk and Kreevich opened it and showed the contents to Headman, dozens of bundles of neatly packed ten-, twenty-, and hundred-dollar bills.

"My God!" Headman said.

"You didn't know what was in the bag, Headman?" Kreevich asked.

"God, no!" Headman said. "He looked tired. I just offered to carry the bag for him."

Kreevich looked at Johnny.

"He asked if he could carry the bag," Johnny said. "I knew what he meant."

"Will you please tell me what this is all about?" Headman asked. He was a handsome young man, but his gay manner was gone. He looked frightened out of his wits.

"Would it be out of order to ask Mr. Headman where he was on Friday morning, and Saturday afternoon and evening, and early Sunday morning?" Quist asked.

"And last night when Eddie got it?" Johnny said.

"I don't understand," Headman said. "I was here, in New York. I haven't been out of the city for weeks."

"You weren't in California last Friday morning?" Kreevich asked.

"I tell you, I haven't been out of the city!"

"You weren't in Chicago on Saturday afternoon and early evening?"

"No!"

"Exactly where were you?"

Headman moistened his lips. "God Almighty! I—I have to think. I've been working with Mrs. Delbert Scheer on the Respiratory Diseases Benefit for the last couple of weeks. Friday? I—I was in her apartment most of the day making phone calls for her."

"And Saturday?"

"Same thing. Last-minute details. I went to the Garden sometime in the early afternoon to check out the arrangements. I had dinner with Mrs. Scheer and then we went to the Garden for the evening."

Kreevich turned to one of his men. "Ask Mrs. Scheer to come over here, Sergeant. We might as well check out these alibis now."

One of the men left the room.

"Will you tell me what it is you think I've done?" Headman pleaded.

"All in good time," Kreevich said.

Quist moved Garvey over to a far corner of the room. "Can you locate your young friend Toby Tyler?" he asked.

"I can try," Garvey said. "What for?"

"Headman could be the guy Tyler described to you— the Chief."

"The bearded weirdo?"

"Anybody can shave off a beard and get a haircut," Quist said.

Headman was allowed to sweat it out while Kreevich waited for Marian Scheer. It was almost an hour before the lady arrived at the precinct house in the company of

Kreevich's man. She had taken time to make herself look attractive. She was ushered into the office where Headman, revived a little by hot coffee, was being held.

"Doug, what on earth—?" she said.

"It's wild," Headman said. "There's some ghastly mistake."

Marian Scheer saw Quist. "Shouldn't Doug have a lawyer, Mr. Quist? I understand it's something about money in a suitcase which he's supposed to have tried to steal from Johnny. That simply doesn't make sense."

"They want to know where I was—" Headman began.

"We'll ask Mrs. Scheer what we want to know," Kreevich said. "Would you mind telling us, Mrs. Scheer, how you spent last Friday?"

"How *I* spent last Friday? What have I got to do with—"

"They want to know what I—" Headman tried again.

"If you don't keep still, Headman, I'll have you removed from the room," Kreevich said. "Please, Mrs. Scheer, if you wouldn't mind telling us about your day on Friday—and Saturday, for that matter."

"Goodness knows it's no secret," Marian Scheer said. "I was—am—chairman of the benefit for the Foundation to Combat Respiratory Diseases. You know we had a benefit at the Garden on Saturday night with Johnny Sands as the chief attraction. There are a thousand details connected with such a do, Lieutenant. Friday? I spent most of the day at home, phoning people, cleaning up last-minute details."

"Alone?"

"Lord, no," Marian Scheer said. "There were dozens of people in and out all day. Doug came right after breakfast and spent most of the day there helping with the phone calls."

" 'Doug' is Mr. Headman?"

"Yes, of course."

"And Saturday?"

"Saturday, as Doug would say, was wild. Phone calls again, in and out. I don't know what I would have done without Doug. He spent the whole day helping. He went to the Garden for me sometime during the afternoon. Took me to dinner and kept me calm. I was a mass of nerves. Then he went to the Garden with me. He took me home after the benefit was over. You may know, Lieutenant, it was well after three in the morning when Johnny finished singing."

"So Headman took you home?"

"Yes, along with two or three other people. We had what you might call breakfast. It must have been about seven o'clock in the morning when it broke up, wasn't it, Doug?"

Headman was smiling. "At least that," he said.

So much for trying to tie Headman into the murders, Quist told himself. Alibi for Friday, alibi for Saturday, alibi for early Sunday morning; other people, 'in and out,' to back those alibis up if that was needed.

Somebody touched Quist's arm. He turned and saw that it was Dan Garvey. He'd been unaware that while Marian Scheer was talking Garvey had slipped into the office with an attractive young man who had a puzzled looked on his face. Garvey beckoned, and Quist went out into the hall with Garvey and his friend.

"Toby Tyler," Garvey said.

"Hi, Mr. Quist."

"Hi."

"Well, Toby, what about it?" Garvey asked. "Is Headman your bearded character from the coast?"

"No way I can answer that," Tyler said, frowning. "Nothing like him at all—jazzy modern suit, tailored, barbered. Maybe about the same size and coloring, but nothing—nothing real. I'd have to say no."

"What's bothering you?" Quist asked. "Just that you wish you could help us and can't?"

"It's the woman in there," Tyler said. "Who is she? Mrs. Scheer?"

"Yes. Society widow. Rich."

"I've seen a picture of her," Tyler said.

"She hits the society pages all the time," Garvey said. "We've all seen pictures of her."

"You won't believe where I saw mine," Tyler said. His smile was forced. "You weren't interested in my private life when we talked, Dan. But I'll let you in on it. I did have my moment with Beverly Trent."

"So you were a member of the club," Garvey said.

"Yeah. And that's where I saw my picture of Mrs. Scheer; in a silver frame on Beverly Trent's bureau."

PART THREE

Chapter 1

"THERE ARE ABSOLUTELY NO GROUNDS on which I can hold him," Kreevich said. He had joined Quist and Garvey and young Toby Tyler in the corridor outside the office where Marian Scheer and Headman waited. He had brought an exhausted-looking Johnny Sands with him. "Sands admits that Headman simply asked if he could carry the bag. He didn't snatch it, or even take it away from him. Sands handed it to him."

"He's the one," Johnny said doggedly. He gave young Tyler a curious look. "Haven't I seen you somewhere before, Tyler?"

Tyler's smile was relaxed. "Around Hollywood," he said. "I once attended a famous champagne party you gave."

Johnny stiffened. "What the hell are you doing here?"

Quist explained that Tyler was a friend of Garvey's and that he had once been Beverly Trent's agent on the Coast. Kreevich knew the whole story; there was nothing to hide.

"Tyler thought he remembered that a man had come to your party with Beverly," Garvey said. "You ever heard of anyone called the Chief, Johnny?"

Johnny frowned. "Some long-haired nut out on the

Coast, isn't he? Had a stable of dames—and one of them burned herself alive at a party Gig Lawson was giving? You think he was at my champagne party, Tyler?"

"I know he was," Tyler said.

Johnny shook his head slowly. "There were people I didn't know at that party. Long hair and beards are nothing new. Could be, I suppose. But what's that got to do with the screwball in the other room?"

"We tried to make a connection, Johnny," Quist said. "If Headman was really after that money then he could also be the killer. He could be the Chief. That's why we were trying to get alibis from him. We brought Tyler here to have a look at him."

"Well, is he or isn't he?" Johnny asked.

"No way I can answer that," Tyler said. "If I didn't know what you wanted me to say, I'd say no."

"Just the truth," Kreevich said.

"I couldn't possibly say yes. About the right height and size, but nothing else. Dark hair, that's all."

"A million guys like that."

"Yes," Tyler said. He looked at Quist. "Is the other thing important?"

"Were you ever in Beverly Trent's apartment, Johnny?" Quist asked. I know you were there the night you and Sabol and Liebman took her body there, but any other time?"

Johnny shook his head. "It was a cheap rat's nest," he said. "I wouldn't want to be seen coming or going. The times Beverly and I were together were at my place."

"Toby spent a night there," Quist said.

"You too?" Johnny said bitterly. "Boy, she really laid 'em end to end."

"Toby saw something there that's rather interesting," Quist said. He glanced at Kreevich. "A photograph in a silver frame. You remember any photographs, Johnny?"

"Look, the night we went there all we wanted to do was hurry," Johnny said. "We put her on the bed, left the pill bottle on the table beside her, and got the hell out of there. Whose picture was it, John Wayne's? Our Beverly went after big shots."

"It was a picture of Marian Scheer," Quist said. A neat bombshell, he thought.

Johnny's mouth sagged. "You're kidding!"

"You're certain of that, Mr. Tyler?" Kreevich asked.

"Positive, Lieutenant."

"Marian has her pictures in the papers all the time," Johnny said.

"Tell me, Toby, was the picture you saw cut out of a newspaper or magazine?" Quist asked.

"No," Tyler said. "It was a regular eight-by-ten studio portrait."

"You knew Mrs. Scheer and you recognized her?" Kreevich asked.

"No. I never saw her till just now in the other room. But that's whose picture it was on Beverly's bureau. No doubt."

"So we ask Marian what Beverly was doing with her picture," Johnny said. He turned toward the office door.

"Cool it for a minute, Johnny," Quist said. He turned to Kreevich. "She's up tight in there, angry. She isn't going to answer questions readily. I'll escort her home, slip it to her without her realizing it's part of your interrogation. You can't hold her either, Lieutenant."

"The Trent case isn't really my business," Kreevich said. "I'm concerned with the murders of Max Liebman and Eddie Wismer. Sands' blackmailer is probably my killer. Looks like he gave us the slip tonight. With this odd bit about Mrs. Scheer I'll check those alibis, but I have a sick feeling they'll hold up. Go ahead, Quist. Try to find out about the picture. It might add up to something." He turned to Johnny. "I want you to go back to Quist's apartment and stay there, Sands. Sergeant Quillan will take you under guard."

"You think I'll hear from the blackmailer again?" Johnny asked.

"He didn't get the money, did he?"

Kreevich told Marian Scheer and Headman they could go. He was sorry for having pulled Headman in, but under the circumstances—

"If you'll let me take you home, Marian, and you'll buy me a drink," Quist said at his charming best, "I'll tell you the whole story."

That faintly predatory look crept into her eyes. "Poor Doug needs to understand what happened to him," she said.

"Glad to try to bring light," Quist said.

"It shouldn't take forever to make things clear to the poor boy," she said archly.

When they came out of the office Johnny, Garvey, and Tyler were gone. Quist got a taxi and they headed for Marian's apartment on the East Side. Young Headman was still in a kind of daze.

"You can't imagine what it was like," he said. "I saw him starting to leave the Garden, with that goddam bag. I hadn't noticed him earlier. I mean, it was quite a game. Something about how tired he looked touched me. It seemed as if the bag was heavy. I just went up to him, and said hello, and asked if I could carry his bag for him to a taxi, or his car, or whatever. He gave me this kind of blank look, handed me the bag, and then he was all over me, fighting like a crazy man. Just instinctively I had to protect myself."

"Johnny had been waiting for somebody to ask him for that bag all night," Quist said. He was sitting between

Marian and Headman. They were both looking at him, eager for answers.

He told them that Johnny was being blackmailed by some kind of a psycho killer. The only thing he left out was the story of Beverly Trent. He explained he wasn't at liberty to tell what it was the blackmailer had on Johnny. He told them about the four murders and their belief that this mysterious madman was either trying to frighten Johnny into resuming payments, or that he would eventually make the attempt to kill Johnny.

"The four men who have been killed, including poor EddieWismer, all knew what it is the blackmailer has on Johnny. So it connects, you see. This morning the blackmailer called Johnny and demanded a hundred thousand dollars—or else. He was to take the money to the Garden in a suitcase and someone would ask him for it. We couldn't understand this method of payoff. The blackmailer must know we could cover Johnny in a crowd like that. I thought he might be setting up Johnny for a sniper. He sat through that whole game, waiting for a bullet to crash into his skull, or for someone to ask him for the bag."

"My God!" Marian said.

"You can imagine how raw his nerves were, Headman, when you walked up to him and offered to relieve him of the bag."

Headman was staring wide-eyed at Quist. "So they were asking me where I was on Friday and Saturday and early Sunday morning because they thought I might be the killer?"

"You asked for the bag," Quist said. "Unfortunately, two and two sometimes make five."

"So now Johnny has to wait for the man to call him again—to ask for money or perhaps to try to kill him?" Marian asked.

"Yes."

"It's simply too awful."

"I don't know what came over me to suggest carrying the bag for him," Headman said. "It was just that he looked so tired. Who was the young man your friend Garvey brought in?"

"We have reason to think the killer-blackmailer may be some sort of a psycho young man who lived out on the Coast. He was known as the Chief. Dan's friend Toby Tyler knew him by sight. In California this Chief fellow was a long-haired, bearded hippie-type. Toby said he reminded him of Charles Manson."

"How horrible," Marian said.

"We thought—since you asked for the bag, Headman; since that suggested you might be the killer—you might be this Chief fellow cleaned up. We brought Toby in to have a look at you."

"And—?"

"Of course he said you weren't the man," Quist said.

Headman let his breath out in a long sigh. "God, how close you can come to total disaster through a coincidence. If I hadn't had the impulse to offer to carry that bag! One of Kreevich's men might have shot me down!"

"If you'd run instead of fighting back," Quist said.

The cab pulled up outside Marian's house. Quist paid for it. In the house they went up to the living room where Quist had first seen Marian. He said, when asked, that he'd like to have a Jack Daniels on the rocks. Headman went to the bar in the far corner to make drinks. Quist sat down in a comfortable armchair and stretched his long legs out in front of him. He was more tired than he'd realized.

"Please smoke one of your cigars," Marian said.

He took one from the case in his pocket and lit it. She placed a small table with an ashtray beside him. In the process she brushed against him. She never stopped the come-on, he thought.

"I was frightened to death when they came for me," she said. "I couldn't imagine what Doug had done. I can't tell you how relieved I was when I saw you there."

"Kreevich is a good man," Quist said. "He did what he had to do." He was wondering how to get around to the question about Beverly Trent, casually. Some instinct warned him against asking it. If the picture tied in with Johnny in some fashion, the question might put Marian on guard.

"Have you ever lived in California?" he asked, taking a contented pull at his cigar.

"I've never even been there," she said.

"Somehow I imagined you as someone who'd traveled everywhere," he said.

"Delbert and I traveled a lot," she said, "but it was always the other way—England, France, Spain, Italy, Greece. Would you believe I've never been farther west in this country than St. Paul? Delbert took me out there on a business trip when we were first married." She smiled faintly. "When we were first married Delbert wouldn't leave me overnight."

"Sensible man."

Headman came back from the bar with drinks. "I suppose whatever trouble Johnny's in is based in California," he said.

"That's a logical guess," Quist said. "He's lived there most of his adult life."

"Is that why you asked me if I'd ever lived in California, Julian?" Marian asked.

It was like an alarm bell ringing in his head now. *Don't ask her about Beverly Trent!*

"I suppose I was wondering if you'd known any of Johnny's crowd on the Coast," he said. "You lived any

135

time in Hollywood, Headman?"

"I spent a week there once," Headman said. "Some week. I was on my college football team and we went out to play Southern Cal. Coach kept us locked up like prisoners."

"What college did you go to?"

"Notre Dame," Headman said. "Oh, I never made any headlines. Third-string end, I was. About all I saw of California was the airport, some country club where we stayed, and the stadium."

Don't ask the question!

Quist finished his drink and stood up. "So help me, I didn't realize how thoroughly bushed I am," he said. "The tensions tonight were really something. If you'll forgive me, Marian, I think I'll toddle off."

"You'll stay in touch, won't you? We'll be dying of curiosity to know what happens," she said.

He sounded grim. "If anything happens to Johnny Sands you'll know," he said.

There was one of Kreevich's men in the lobby of the Beekman Place apartment building, another in the corridor outside Quist's front door. Quist let himself into the apartment and was pleased to see Lydia stretched out on his couch. She sat up and came to him. He kissed her gently.

"Johnny?" he asked.

"Gone to bed in the study with a bottle of Irish." She smiled. "After making a polite pass at me. I thought he looked relieved when I regretted. He's done in, poor guy. Make you a drink?"

He nodded. "I had a Jack Daniels where I was."

She went over to the bar. "How did it go?"

"I'm damned if I know how to answer that," he said. "I went there to ask her a question and I didn't ask it."

"Why not?"

"Ghost walked over my grave—I don't know, honestly
—something kept telling me not to. Getting old-woman-
ish, I guess."

She brought him his drink and wandered away toward
the open doors to the terrace. "Julian?" she said.

"Yes, love."

"What is an Indian chief? I mean what's his position?"

"He's the king, the boss, the head man," Quist said.

Lydia turned, her violet eyes wide. "Just remember you
said it, not me, darling."

"Said what?"

"Head man," she said.

He stared at her.

"Didn't Dan say this creep on the Coast was named
David Harris?" she asked.

"I think so."

"D. H.—David Harris," she said. "Initials. D. H.—
Douglas Headman." She let her breath out in a quavering
little sigh. "I can't think of any more coincidences,
Julian."

He stood very still, staring at her. "Word games," he
said.

"Why didn't you ask Marian Scheer if she knew Beverly Trent?"

"I tell you, something warned me not to."

"Douglas Headman is cleared," Lydia said. "His alibis
will stand up, even if you have doubts about Mrs. Scheer.
There were many other people around those days for
which he needed an alibi. He isn't the murderer. He apparently isn't the blackmailer."

"So?"

"So we forget about him," Lydia said.

"Except for your word game. Head man—Headman."
Quist wandered restlessly over to the bar and freshened

137

his drink.

"There must be perfectly innocent reasons why Beverly Trent would have had a picture of Marian Scheer in her room."

"Name two," Quist said.

"A rich society woman; someone Beverly admired, maybe wanted to use as a model."

"A studio photograph, not a newspaper clipping," Quist said.

"Oh, come on, darling. You know how easy it is to get photographs of people from photographers, other sources."

"What other sources?"

"Maybe she wrote Mrs. Scheer and asked for it."

"So that's one innocent reason. Name another, love."

Lydia hesitated. "I can't think of one, but there must be others."

"Head man," Quist said. "Chief. You stinker."

"Well, what's to worry, Julian? He's cleared."

Quist wandered over to the terrace doors and stared out into the night. Lydia followed him after a moment and stood beside him, her arm linked in his.

"What's bothering you, Julian?"

"I'm thinking about that goddamned top hat," he said.

"Top hat?"

"Chambrun's top hat with the false bottom." Quist turned and looked at her. "I think that's what stopped me from asking Marian Scheer about the photograph. Something about her, and about Headman."

"What—aside from my silly coincidences?"

He turned and looked down at her. His pale blue eyes were contracted, cold. "I was sure no one would ever collect that bag of money at the Garden," he said. "There was absolutely no way to get away with it. That's why I came up with the sniper theory."

"Fortunately you were wrong."

"So what did happen? What was the purpose of that whole charade?"

"Nothing happened."

"Wrong. Douglas Headman was cleared of all suspicion of murder and blackmail."

"So?"

"So the next time the blackmailer calls there is one person we won't be watching. Douglas Headman. He's clean. Magic trick. Our attention is called to him, he's cleared, so we don't watch him again—and out of the hat comes the rabbit."

"But the alibis."

"Provided by someone who has a connection with the starting point of this whole horror. Those alibis need a more thorough checking." He reached down and touched her cheek. "Go home and get some rest. In the morning we start digging for the real truth about your head man and his lady friend."

It was unspokenly understood that Lydia would not stay the night with Quist. With Johnny sleeping in the study it would be, somehow, less than private. There was a small debate as to whether Quist should walk the two blocks to Lydia's apartment with her. She convinced him that someone should stay by Johnny. It was an unusually well-policed area. Lydia felt no fear. She would phone him the minute she got home.

Quist made himself a nightcap and waited. In less than ten minutes Lydia called.

"Safe and sound," she said. "Get some sleep."

"I'll try."

"I already miss you," Lydia said.

Quist switched off lights and went upstairs to his sleeping quarters. He slid out of clothes, feeling almost somambulistic. God, he was tired.

He slept at once.

And woke up with the sound of screaming in his ears.

It took him a moment to orient himself, and then he realized that the cries of terror were coming from Johnny Sands on the floor below. He sprang out of bed and ran into his dressing room. He pulled on a yellow terrycloth robe and, from the top drawer of his dresser, hidden under a pile of handkerchiefs, he took a .38-caliber police special.

He raced down the stairs and into the study. The screaming had stopped. In the half light from behind him Quist saw Johnny sitting bolt upright in bed.

"Johnny!"

"Oh, God!" Johnny moaned.

"I'm turning on the light," Quist said, and flipped the switch by the door. He stood in the full light, sweeping the room with his gun, looking for some movement behind drapes.

"Was I yelling?" Johnny asked in a husky voice.

"Jesus, man!"

Johnny was squinting sleep-heavy eyes against the light. "So you did have a hand gun," he said. "It's a good thing you didn't give it to me. I'd have killed that Headman."

"Johnny, what's wrong?"

"Bad dream," Johnny said. He fumbled on the side table for a cigarette.

"You scared the hell out of me," Quist said. He slipped the gun into the pocket of his robe.

Johnny got his cigarette lit and reached for the bottle of Irish whiskey that was on the floor beside his bed. "Somebody was trying to kill me—with a silver candlestick," he said.

"If you weren't so full of hootch I'd offer you a sleeping pill," Quist said. He turned back toward the door.

"Don't go," Johnny said with a kind of urgency. "Stay and talk to me, pal."

"I'm dead on my feet," Quist said. "Tomorrow's going to be a busy day."

"What's with tomorrow?"

"Just to satisfy myself I'm going to do a little further checkout on Headman and your girl friend, Marian."

"You mean Headman could still be it?"

"Tonight it seems just remotely possible," Quist said. "Tomorrow it may evaporate into smoke. Try not to have any more bad dreams, will you?"

Johnny waved the whiskey bottle and gave Quist a lop-sided grin. "Do my best, pal."

Chapter 2

"There are things about Master Headman," Quist said. He was in a huddle in his office with Lydia, Garvey, and Connie Parmalee. "To begin with, he's not in the telephone book."

Garvey was his usual sour self. "I prefer you, Julian, when you are being rational," he said. "So Lydia comes up with what you call word games, and coincidences, and suddenly alibis don't check for you. He has the same initials as David Harris. Look in the phone book and I'll bet you come up with two dozen guys who have the initials D.H. So he isn't in the book, so he gave Kreevich all his vital statistics last night; name, address, phone number. Then you talk about top hats! So help me, Julian—"

"Why did the blackmailer set up an impossible drop for the money?" Quist asked cheerfully.

"I don't know. But it doesn't have anything to do with Headman. He cleared himself to Kreevich's satisfaction. So stop playing magic games. You've got trouble enough keeping Johnny covered and dealing with the real blackmailer when he shows again."

Quist reached for one of his cigars. "Headman told me he was a third-string end on the Notre Dame varsity football team," he said. "Made a trip to the Coast for a game with Southern Cal. You know people at Notre Dame, don't you, Daniel? Let's find out what they remember about him."

"What can they tell you?"

"Who knows, Daniel. You object to calling some friend out there and asking?"

Garvey muttered something under his breath and picked up the phone. "I want to get a Patrick O'Mara at Notre Dame University, South Bend," he told the operator. "Yes, person to person." He hung up. "What year did Headman play?" he asked.

"No idea," Quist said. "He's under thirty, wouldn't you say? Five, six, seven years ago would be about right."

"We supply the haystack, O'Mara produces the needle." Garvey lit a cigarette and glared at the telephone, daring his friend O'Mara to come on.

"While we're waiting," Quist said, "I'd like to dig into the history of Mrs. Delbert Scheer; who she was before she married Scheer in 1962, where she comes from, the works. Society reporters can give you something, I'm sure. Who was she before she married a man old enough to be her father? Where did she spring from originally? Who took studio photographs of her, one of which drifted into the hands of Beverly Trent, dead now for five years? Lydia, you and Connie go to work on that, will you?"

The phone rang. Quist leaned forward and switched on the squawk box. He gestured to Garvey.

"I have Mr. O'Mara for you," the switchboard operator said.

"Pat? Dan Garvey here," Garvey said.

"How are you, you old bastard?"

"Fine. Need your help with something."

"Shoot."

"A few years ago—five-six, maybe seven years ago—you had a kid named Douglas Headman who played end on

143

the varsity football team. Third string, from what I hear.

"Headman? I don't remember a Headman."

"The year he was on the team you played Southern California on the Coast. Team put up at some country club out there."

"Nineteen sixty-six would fit that," O'Mara said. "But I don't remember any Headman. I would remember, too, Dan, because I was assisting with the offensive linemen that year. No Headman."

"I must have had a bum steer," Garvey said.

O'Mara laughed. "I do remember, God knows, a third-string end that year. Fellow named Hirsch—Don Hirsch. He skipped the team after the game. We had the State Police and the FBI looking for him. Thought something had happened to him. Turned out he'd just decided to quit school without telling anyone. Turned up living in some crazy commune out there; long-haired guys, ready and willing girls."

"What did this Hirsch look like? Can you remember?" Garvey's voice had tightened.

"Oh, I remember, all right. Six feet—light weight, about a hundred and sixty pounds—black hair. He had a lot of moxie, but he really wasn't fast enough or big enough."

"They'd have a record on him out there, wouldn't they, Pat? Where he came from, all that? Hirsch, I mean."

"Dean's office. I could dig it up for you if it's important. You think he's your Headman?"

"Could be. It could be very important, Pat."

"Okay. Call me back toward the end of the day. Four-five o'clock. Nice to talk to you, Dan boy."

"I'll be calling," Garvey said.

The phone clicked off. Garvey stood staring at Quist, his face a dark thundercloud.

"Don Hirsch, initials D.H.," Lydia said in a small voice.

"Hippie commune," Quist said. His eyes were narrowed, his smile thin. "Maybe our Mr. Headman let his foot slip a little when he mentioned Notre Dame football. Maybe we've just heard of the beginnings of the Chief." He pushed a button on his desk. "Ask Gloria to get someone to take over for her. I'd like to talk to her in here."

Connie stood up. "Let me get on the Scheer trail," she said, and went off to her own office.

"I have to admit there are a hell of a lot too many coincidences about this," Garvey said.

Miss Gloria Chard, the receptionist, looking dazzling, came into the office.

"What have I done?" she asked.

"You had lunch with Douglas Headman yesterday," Quist said.

"But you told me it was okay!" Gloria said. She looked apprehensively at Lyida.

Quist smiled at her. "I did and it was," he said. "But young Mr. Headman interests us. What did you find out about him, love?"

Gloria lowered her extra-long eyelashes. "Not very much about him," she said. "I did find out that I was the most beautiful, most desirable creature on earth, and that unless I said yes to everything he asked he would, almost certainly, go mad, mad, mad."

"Pleasantly reassuring," Quist said, "But didn't he say anything about himself?"

"Only that if I said yes I would discover that I'd never really known what love-making could be."

"And would it be too personal to ask whether you did say yes or not?" Quist asked, still smiling.

Gloria looked up at him. "I said 'maybe.' He's a darned attractive guy, Mr. Quist. I'm supposed to have dinner with him tonight."

"Under his head of steam why did he skip last night?"

145

Quist asked.

"He was desolate, he said, but he had an unbreakable engagement. Business."

"A date to be at Madison Square Garden," Garvey muttered.

That went by Gloria. "If there's some reason I shouldn't see him, Mr. Quist, of course I'll—"

"Don't rush your fences, Gloria," Quist said. "I can only tell you that Headman may have something more to him than his talents as a Casanova. Do you know where he lives?"

"He's subletting an apartment from someone on the East Side."

"Is that where your date is for tonight?"

"If I keep it."

"A sublet explains his absence from the phone book," Garvey said.

"Didn't you get a hint as to what he does?" Quist asked. "Does he work at something? Does he have a job?"

"He told me he was a promoter."

"Promoter of what?"

"He didn't say. Really, Mr. Quist, there was nothing to our luncheon but a whirlwind assault on my—on my feminine charms."

"Whatever else we may think of your Mr. Headman he has taste. First Lydia, and then you." Quist tapped his slender fingers on the edge of his desk. "There's something curious about Headman, maybe dangerous. I'm not sure you should keep your date."

"She damn well shouldn't," Garvey said.

Gloria glanced at Garvey. She looked pleased. Office scuttlebutt had it that Miss Chard had long had her cap set for Mr. Garvey.

Quist leaned forward. "I want to know what he

'promotes,'" he said. "I want to know where he came from originally. I want to know how long he's lived in New York. I want to know when he changed his name from Hirsch to Harris, and when he changed his name from Harris to Headman."

Gloria's eyes were wide. "I don't understand," she said. "Is he some kind of—of—"

"He is," Garvey said.

"I think perhaps Gloria should know the whole story," Quist said. "Take her somewhere, Lydia, and brief her. Then come back to me, Gloria. When you know the whole scoop we can discuss whether or not you keep your date."

The two girls left for Lydia's office.

"So there may be something to your theory," Garvey said. "The whole thing at the Garden was set up to turn our attention away from Headman. If he is the Chief— Hirsch—Harris—"

"Johnny will be hearing soon again," Quist said. "This time the delivery of the money will be hard to stop."

"He still isn't the killer," Garvey said.

"If his alibis do, in fact, hold up. This is a very smooth operator, Daniel, and if there is anything at all fishy about Marian Scheer those alibis may not stand a closer look."

"Promoter!" Garvey said angrily. "He's promoting a hundred thousand bucks from Johnny."

"And if we're right that brings his total over a quarter of a million," Quist said. "Nice work if you can get it."

"Gloria shouldn't keep that date," Garvey said. "If this guy is the Chief, God knows what kind of sadistic pleasures may be involved."

Quist studied the end of his cigar. "My guess is that Gloria can handle Mr. Headman."

"So what's our next move?" Garvey asked. "You tell Kreevich you detect a false bottom in Headman's top hat?"

"I tell him. He may or may not buy it. I'm inclined to wait till we have more facts. Your man at Notre Dame may turn up something on Hirsch. Gloria may turn up something on Headman."

"Meanwhile Headman sets up a new rendezvous with Johnny and takes off for the moon with a suitcase full of money."

"He may try," Quist agreed. "He'll phone Johnny with instructions. This time the delivery will take place somewhere Johnny can't possibly be covered by Kreevich—without Headman knowing."

"So he gets away with it. Johnny drops the bag somewhere; Headman won't show this time till Johnny's gone."

Quist nodded. "He'll be watching Johnny to make sure he isn't covered by Kreevich. But there's one thing he won't be watching for, Daniel."

"What's that?"

"He won't be watching for anyone who might be covering *him*. He's in the clear, alibied, whistling down the middle of the street. No reason why anyone should be watching him. So we pick him up and we stay with him. We persuade Kreevich to call off his dogs. Johnny delivers the money, and when Headman moves in to collect it we grab him."

" 'We?' "

Quist smiled. "I was thinking of you, Daniel," he said.

The day moved on slowly, with nothing new to add to the puzzle. There were clients Quist had to see if he wasn't to go out of business. The only thing of consequence was a brief session with Gloria Chard.

"I'm not afraid to keep my date with Headman," she told Quist.

"It could be enormously helpful," Quist said. "You may get some of the information we need. But there is one other thing. If he's involved with you, love, he won't be up to anything else. It will give us a little time. It may be that before tonight we'll know enough to let you break the date."

Her smile was tentative.

Quist showed mock concern. "What has he got that I haven't got?"

Her eyes brightened. "You ask me for a date, boss, and I'll drop Mr. Headman like a hot cake."

"You've made my day," he said. "Run along, love. We'll let you know toward the end of the day where the wind blows."

It was toward the end of the afternoon that Connie Parmalee, her amber-tinted glasses neatly in place on her very nice nose, came into the office with a sheaf of notes.

"When you want, I have a preliminary on Marian Scheer," she said.

"I want," he said.

She sat down in the chair beside his desk. He had learned to look away from the handsome expanse of leg revealed by her miniskirt.

"Some of this may surprise you a little," she said. "It goes backwards, if you don't mind, since I had to work it backwards."

"Play it your way, love," Quist said.

"Delbert Scheer died in 1966—December. He was seventy-two years old. Had a heart attack on the way to his office. He was a stock broker, seat on the exchange. Owned the house on Eightieth Street where the lady lives.

"Fascinating," Quist said dryly. He reached for a cigar

149

and lit it.

"More fascinating than you might think," Connie said. "Mr. Scheer was on the verge of bankruptcy when he died. Broke, in short. The Eightieth Street house mortgaged to the hilt. The word broke is relative, of course. He left the house, with its mortgage, to Marian. In a private account, set up for Marian before Delbert died, was about forty thousand dollars. The rest of his estate, also left to her, was zero.

"How do you like that!"

"Business obligations she wasn't forced legally to pay. So she had the mortgaged house and forty thousand dollars. To keep up the payments on the interest and principal and to maintain her style of living our Marian could look forward to a shortish future."

"Where did you get all this, Connie?"

"Teddy Murack at your bank. He owes you a favor. She was just about reaching the bottom of the barrel in the spring of '69 when she had some kind of a windfall. Like fifty thousand dollars was suddenly deposited to her account. A year later, the same thing. Another fifty thousand. Suggest anything to you, boss?"

Quist's eyes were narrow slits. "Beverly Trent died in '68. The blackmailing started in '69 and carried through '70."

"Same thing occurred to me," Connie said. "Of course I can't connect her deposits with the blackmail. Just a coincidence."

"Keep cooking," Quist said.

"Our Marian married Delbert Scheer in 1962. She was a widow at the time, aged thirty-two according to the marriage license. Her late husband was Mike Daniels, a society playboy. You may remember him; polo, night clubs, big splurger. He and Marian traveled, raised public hell. They were part of the jetset of their day. Mike was killed in an airplane crash in '61. He didn't leave Marian very well fixed. It turned out he'd been living off his family. They blew Marian to a two-room apartment off Gramercy Park and I suspect gave her a small allowance. In less than a year she hooked Delbert Scheer and apparent security forever.

"According to Johnny she has hooking talents," Quist said.

"It's only just getting interesting," Connie said.

"Go."

"Nobody seems to know very much about Marian before she met Mike Daniels. Among other things Mike Daniels was a championship ski jumper. He went out West for a meet in 1957. St. Paul, to be exact. He came back with a beautiful bride. Nobody ever heard of or met any family of hers. According to Sally Blaine, my society reporter friend, a lot of the debutante cats who'd had their eyes on Mike Daniels said she was a nothing. They whispered that she had been a waitress, a hat-check girl, a call girl. She lived it down, whatever the truth.

"So, like I said, she has talents."

"That's not what's so interesting," Connie said. "I just finished checking with St. Paul—records in the town hall. Sure enough, Mike Daniels was married out there in '57. Care to guess the bride's name?"

"Marian," Quist said.

"That's half a bull's-eye," Connie said. Her eyes were fixed steadily on Quist. "Hold on to your hat, boss. The bride's name was Marian Hauptmann."

Quist sat bolt upright in his chair. "God save us!" he said.

"The world of coincidence," Connie said. "Beverly Trent, Louise Hauptmann. Marian Scheer, Marian Hauptmann."

"Beverly Trent, according to Dan's friend Tyler, came

out of an orphanage in St. Paul," Quist said. "One has to guess she was in her twenties when she killed herself, which means she predates Marian's marriage to Mike Daniels by quite a little. She's been dead for five years. That puts her birth back toward the end of World War II."

"Marian Scheer is forty-two," Connie said, "if the age given on her marriage license for her marriage to Scheer is right. She would have been fifteen, sixteen, seventeen, when Beverly was born."

"Old enough to be a mother," Quist said. "Wartime promiscuity; it could be. It would explain dropping a baby on the orphanage's doorstep."

"It would explain why Beverly had a picture of Marian Scheer on her bureau," Connie said.

Quist pushed back his chair and began to prowl the office, Connie watching him through her tinted glasses. "Let's assume that we're right about Marian and Beverly," Quist said. "And let's assume that we're right in saying that Douglas Headman is the Chief. Beverly, according to Tyler, was one of the Chief's squaws for a while. He had his girls hypnotized, according to Tyler. They would do anything he asked—like setting fire to themselves at a party. They would tell him anything he asked. 'Who are you, dear? Where do you come from? What about your family?' He would be interested in prying a fast buck out of anyone he could. He finds out that Beverly's mother is a rich society widow who isn't anxious to recognize Beverly as her child. A source of revenue, except that when he gets around to it Marian is broke. Marian is broke and Beverly is dead. Marian can't pay for silence; Marian needs dough as much as he does. And so—"

"They become a team," Connie said.

"Right. Interesting to know how, but the figures support it. Fifty thousand dollars appear in Marian's account for two successive years, the two years Johnny paid blackmail. That's half of what he paid. Headman had something on her, she had something on him."

"What?"

Quist shrugged. "Maybe he told her too much in trying to twist her arm. He was the Chief. The police want him in the case of the girl who burned herself alive. So they join forces to get what they both need—money. Johnny is the victim."

"And so far we can't prove any of it," Connie said.

"Bear one thing in mind, love," Quist said. "Kreevich has to build a case the D.A. can make stand up in court. We don't. Headman has alibis for the murder and Kreevich has to accept them. We don't. They've managed them somehow, faked them."

"But what do we do?"

"Dan and I have already set a trap for Headman. He'll approach Johnny again, and when he does we've got him."

"And Mrs. Scheer?"

"I think perhaps I can throw the fear of God into her so that she'll make Headman hurry—and it will be over with."

"You'll be careful, boss, won't you?" Connie said. Her voice wasn't quite steady. "This man kills without stopping to draw a deep breath. He chopped down Eddie Wismer and was back at Marian's party minutes later, ready to greet you, smiling and smiling. If you put the squeeze on them—"

"Headman and Marian Scheer don't frighten me," Quist said.

"Then you're not bright," Connie said, her voice sharp.

Quist's face clouded. "I've just now come to the conclusion that you're right, love," he said. "I'm not bright. Not bright at all."

"Meaning?"

He was silent for a moment, his face set in marble-hard lines. Then he seemed to come out of it, smiled at her. "Meaning—thanks for doing a wonderful job, Connie. A call should be put in to Dan's friend at Notre Dame to find out what the Dean's office revealed about Donald Hirsch. Make it, will you, like an angel? Tell Mr. O'Mara that Dan's tied up."

"Where is Dan?"

"Tied up," Quist said, grinning at her. "I'm going home to make sure Johnny's all in one piece. Call me there when you have anything."

Chapter 3

Johnny was a caged lion, and a little drunk. There had probably never been a time before in his life when he hadn't been free to do exactly what he pleased. To be shut in Quist's apartment with policemen back door and front had worn him down.

"I can't take much more of this," he said, when Quist arrived. "You know, I never watched television all day long before. What junk they have! You wouldn't believe it."

"I try not even to think about it," Quist said. He went over to the bar and poured himself a drink. He saw that Johnny was into his second bottle of Irish.

"When is this bastard going to make a move?" Johnny asked.

"Not tonight. He's occupied tonight. You can go to bed with a good book."

"You still think it may be Headman?"

"I do," Quist said. "He has a date with Gloria Chard tonight. I don't think even a hundred grand will take him away from that."

Johnny perched on the arm of a chair, swinging a leg, half-empty drink in one hand, cigarette in the other. "I've been thinking," he said.

"Dangerous occupation," Quist said.

"If Headman's the blackmailer, pal, then we're after two guys. Headman and the killer." Johnny tried a laugh. "If the killer gets to me first the joke will be on Headman."

"The killer isn't going to get to you, Johnny," Quist said. "What's going to happen is that you will get a message to deliver the money somewhere—deliver it without being covered by Kreevich or anyone else. You'll obey orders."

"And goodbye a hundred Gs," Johnny said.

"You won't be covered," Quist said, "but Headman will. He thinks he's in the clear so he won't imagine that anybody will be watching him. Dan's on his tail right now."

"Hey, that's pretty slick."

"After we've caught him we'll find out whether his alibis for the killings really stand up."

"Marian made him look pretty clean," Johnny said.

"Which brings me to Marian," Quist said.

Johnny chuckled. "Don't let anything 'bring' you to Marian, pal," he said. "I warn you, she's good enough so that she might destroy your happy, unmarried life."

"Let's be serious, friend," Quist said. "You know that Tyler saw a picture of Marian on Beverly Trent's bureau in Hollywood."

"I know he says so. Crazy, man."

"Johnny, think. During your fling with Beverly did she ever mention Marian Scheer?"

Johnny sipped his drink. "I don't think so," he said. "I have to explain something to you about Beverly. She was a beautiful hunk of stuff; really, something like you dream about. I've seen the best in my time, pal, and she was the best—to look at." He shook his head as if he couldn't believe a memory. "She was like vaccinated with a phonograph needle. Talk, talk, talk. Right in the middle

of making love to her she'd ask me what I thought about
the war in Vietnam. 'You know what I'd like?' she'd say,
and I, ready to make her happy any way she asked,
would say, 'Name it, baby,' And she'd say, 'I'd love an an-
chovy pizza!' Boy! I finally learned to shut it out. I didn't
hear anything she ever said to me. If she mentioned Marian I didn't hear it, like I didn't hear almost anything she
said."

"She never talked about her family? Her mother?"

"If she did, I didn't hear it," Johnny said. His eyes wid-
ened. "Are you saying Marian might be Beverly's old
lady?" Johnny slipped off the arm of the chair and into it,
convulsed with laughter. "She sure didn't do right by our
Bev if she is. If Marian taught Beverly what she knows
our Beverly could have slept her way right into Buck-
ingham Palace."

"In your moments with Marian she never mentioned
Beverly, or you never mentioned Beverly?"

Johnny stopped laughing. "I haven't mentioned Beverly to anyone for a long time. I wanted people to forget
I ever had anything to do with her. You can understand
that."

The phone rang. It was Connie.

"Hold on to your hat, boss," she said. "Donald Hirsch
won a competitive examination scholarship to Notre
Dame. He came from St. Paul. His parents died when he
was a very small boy and he was brought up by a wid-
owed aunt. The aunt's name was Mrs. August Hauptmann. Shall I go on?"

"Let me guess," Quist said. He sounded grim. "Mrs.
August Hauptmann had a daughter named Marian."

"Bingo," Connie said.

A few minutes before seven Garvey called.

"I've finally made connections with our friend," he said.

"Good," Quist said.

"He's taken Gloria to dinner at The Four Seasons. Nothing cheap about him."

"Some odds and ends here," Quist said casually. "Marian Scheer may have been Beverly Trent's mother. Douglas Headman may have been Donald Hirsch who played end on the Notre Dame football team and skipped college to live in a commune. The Chief, it would seem. He was brought up by an aunt whose married name was Hauptmann. Marian's maiden name was Hauptmann. She could be a sort of cousin of Headman's."

"Wow!" Garvey said. Then, under his breath: "Brothers and sisters have I none, but that man's father is my father's son. Who is he?'"

"Stay with him, Daniel," Quist said.

"Count on it."

A little before eight that evening a thunderstorm hit the city with sudden violence. Quist, who had been walking east on Eightieth Street, ducked into the vestibule of a small shop, closed for the night. There had been a dozen large drops of rain and then the deluge. Lightning streaked the sky in jagged patterns.

Diagonally across the street he could see lights in the windows of Marian Scheer's house. The storm, he told himself, had given him time to reconsider. He hadn't wanted to forewarn Marian of a visit. If she and Headman were linked together, as he believed, he didn't want Headman alerted. Headman was occupied with Gloria, and it wasn't likely he'd be contacting Marian. It was an opportunity to apply a little pressure without the allies getting together. He thought he understood Marian Scheer and what made her tick; that there was a chance to break her down and keep Johnny from running the risks of facing Headman in a showdown. If Garvey lost the trail for any reason, the danger to Johnny was great.

The storm swept away over the city almost as rapidly as it had come, leaving the street soaked, flooded at its gutters, lights glittering in the wet.

Quist dodged through the overhang drip from the building where he had taken cover and crossed the street to Marian's house. A uniformed maid opened the door to him. She recognized him.

"I'll tell Mrs. Scheer you're here," she said.

"She doesn't expect me," Quist said. "If she's tied up—"

The maid disappeared into what was obviously a service area. She appeared almost at once, which suggested a house intercom system.

"If you'll go up to the third floor, sir," she said, indicating the elevator.

Marian, looking flushed with pleasure, was waiting for him. She was wearing a wine-red housecoat that was a perfect color for her. Ever-ready, Quist thought.

"I hope you don't mind my dropping in unannounced," he said.

"My dear Julian, I couldn't be more pleased. I was sitting here wondering what to do with my evening. Come in. May I get you a brandy, or do you have another choice?"

"Brandy would be fine," he said.

She was not disconcerted, showed no signs of anxiety. She obviously took his presence to mean that he had understood and responded to certain flirtatious signals she had given him on his other visits. Her eyes were bright with a special excitement as she brought him brandy in a brandy glass; her hand touched his as she gave it to him. She indicated the comfortable armchair he had occupied on another occasion. She noticed little raindrop stains on his pale blue jacket.

"You were caught in the storm?"

159

"Ducked into a vestibule across the street," he said.

"I have always been terrified of lightning," she said. "I'd have been frightened to death if I'd been out in it. But Julian, tell me, is there any news—about Johnny Sands and his problems? That's why you came, isn't it?" She arched an eyebrow. "To bring me news?"

"News of a sort," he said smiling. "Other things that may not be news."

"Oh?"

"There's a great deal of complaint about the police these days," he said. "Increase in crime, and all that. But actually a good police officer, like Lieutenant Kreevich, would surprise you with his thoroughness. They check and check and check, every single detail."

"The Lieutenant impressed me," she said. Her guard was down, Quist thought.

"He's still checking on every last detail of Douglas Headman's story."

She laughed. "Poor Doug. You have no idea what a shocking experience that was for him. As for the Lieutenant, he's been here today, making absolutely certain about Doug's alibis for those ghastly murders."

"Was he satisfied?"

"Of course. I was able to produce five or six people who saw Doug here on Friday and Saturday. The Lieutenant assured me that he was satisfied and that he wouldn't have to bother us anymore."

"Still, there are one or two things about Headman that need clearing," Quist said, still smiling.

For the first time he saw a tightening at the corners of her mouth. "So far as I know Doug is an open book," she said.

"How long have you known him?"

"Doug? Four or five years."

"How did he come your way, Marian?"

She hesitated a moment. "I honestly don't remember. Some party somewhere." Again the arched eyebrows. "He was very flattering to an older woman. I'm not immune, Julian, to men who find me attractive."

"Why should you be?"

"Somehow, Doug became a part of my life—in and out —parties. I do a lot of charity work, you know. Not just the Respiratory Diseases thing. He helped, he ran errands, he made himself useful. I might say indispensable. He's a charming, cultivated, attractive boy. You've heard gossip about him and me?"

"No."

"Well, there has been some, I suppose. My world is populated by cats." She laughed, still at ease.

"Where did he come from, do you know? Where did he originate?"

"I don't really know," she said. "He went to Notre Dame. I remember he told you that. I assumed he came from the Midwest somewhere, but that doesn't make any sense, does it? People from all parts of the country go to Notre Dame."

"Would it surprise you to know that there is no record of his having attended Notre Dame?"

Marian was holding a drink in her right hand. Her left closed so tightly on the arm of her chair that her knuckles were marble-white knobs. "I don't believe you," she said.

"In my business," Quist said, "we're accustomed to people changing their names. Half the people in the theater and films have changed their names. Politicians, even businessmen change their names. I sometimes think there are more people with changed names than those who still use the ones that were pronounced at their christenings. There is no record of a 'Douglas Headman' at Notre Dame, so I wondered if you knew if he had started out in the world with some other handle?"

"If he did he never told me," she said. She sounded suddenly a little breathless.

"What he said about his football career made us wonder if he had started out in life as Donald Hirsch," Quist said.

"If he did he never told me," she said, sharp and quick.

Quist cupped his brandy glass in both hands, warming it. "There was a Donald Hirsch who played third-string end at Notre Dame—did make the trip to California to play in a game there. I wondered. No crime to change your name."

"He never mentioned it," Marian said.

"This Donald Hirsch came from St. Paul," Quist said. His pale blue eyes were suddenly fixed hard on her. "He was a bright boy; won a scholarship to Notre Dame in a competitive examination. It seems his parents died when he was a small boy, and he was raised by an aunt. The aunt's name was Mrs. August Hauptmann."

The color slowly drained from her face. Her eyes looked glassy.

"Mrs. Hauptmann had a daughter whose name, by a strange coincidence, was Marian," Quist said. "This Marian Hauptmann married a man named Mike Daniels. He was killed in a plane crash, and Marian Daniels then married—"

"All right!" She was on her feet, her whole body shaking.

"I haven't finished, Marian," he said quietly. "It's not going to be a secret forever, so I see no reason not to tell you. The trouble Johnny is in has to do with a girl named Beverly Trent. She committed suicide about five years ago. It isn't known, except to a few of us and the police, that the girl killed herself in Johnny's house. He and two friends moved her body to her apartment. Somebody knew this, and that somebody is the person who has been blackmailing Johnny."

Marian was a rigid statute.

"Did I mention that Beverly Trent was one of the changed-name crowd? Her real name was Louise Hauptmann."

"Oh God!" Marian whispered.

"Would it surprise you, Marian, to know that in the girl's apartment was a photograph in a silver frame—a photograph of you?"

She sank very slowly down into her chair. The glass slipped out of her grasp and spilled onto the rug. She lifted her hands to cover her face.

"I hate to open up old wounds," Quist said, turning the brandy glass round in his hands. "I don't like to upset any human being's security. But I am committed to help a friend whose security has been threatened, who has been tortured, who has seen friends close and dear to him murdered in cold blood, who finds himself in the clutches of some psychotic leech. I believe that Douglas Headman is the genius behind the attempted destruction of Johnny Sands. And I'm afraid I believe that you are, in some way, a party to Headman's schemes."

She wavered like a tree about to fall. "I—I think I'm going to be ill," she said. "If you'll excuse me for a moment—"

"I don't think there will be much point in trying to telephone Headman," he said, his voice cold. "He's very much involved tonight with an attractive young girl from my office. I don't think he'll answer a phone call."

She paused in the doorway, holding on to it for support. The physical energy that made her attractive seemed to have drained out of her as if a plug had been pulled.

"What are you going to do?" she asked.

"First, I'm going to talk to you, if you'll let me," Quist

said. "Why don't you make yourself another drink and sit down again?"

She looked at him with eyes that were dark with fear. Then she walked unsteadily to the far end of the room and poured herself another brandy. She came back and stood behind her chair, gripping the back of it with one hand.

"Whatever else," she said, "Doug is not guilty of murder."

"That you know of."

"Not guilty!"

Quist's very relaxation made him seem dangerous to the frightened woman. "Let me begin by saying that I may even feel some sympathy for you, Marian. I may be able to give you a chance without throwing you to the wolves—if you'll help."

"How?"

"I've created a picture of you in my own mind which may be entirely false," he said. "I see you, a young girl, brought up in a fatherless home in a Midwestern city with few if any advantages. I see you becoming a woman in your very early teens, on fire with physical needs and hungers. I see a young soldier on leave, about to take off for Europe, or the Pacific. I see you readily giving him what he asks for because you want it too. A night, a week of dizzying excitement. Then he's gone and you find yourself pregnant. I don't know what position your mother took. I don't know why you went ahead and had the baby."

"I thought he was coming back," she whispered. "I thought it was more than sex. I thought it was love."

"Then there was a 'dear Jane' letter? He was already married?"

She nodded. "It was too late then to—to change my mind."

"And so you had the baby girl, and you left her on the steps of the orphanage. You were what—sixteen—seventeen?"

"Sixteen."

"One of the problems was the baby boy your mother had taken into the family—her nephew, Donald Hirsch. He would have been three—four years old? Your mother, I'm guessing, was outraged with you. She turned all her love and affection to the baby boy. What happened? You left home? Started to make your own way? What ways were there? Waitress, hat-check girl, maybe a defense factory. You had needs that had been awakened in you and had to be satisfied."

"You seem to have checked very thoroughly," she said bitterly, "so you know that I became a high-class call girl."

"I guessed," he said. "After a while there came a customer named Mike Daniels. You were so exciting to him that he was willing to marry you, take you into a whole new world. You wiped St. Paul, and your mother, and your baby cousin out of your life. You made it fine; you had three or four years of that and then your husband was killed and left you flat broke. Then you found what looked like a real gold mine in Delbert Scheer. He was old, but you had the gifts to make him feel like a man again." Quist hesitated. "You know, Marian, I have all kinds of sympathy for you up to now in this story. It's what comes next that I'm concerned about. When did Don-baby come back into your life? Because Douglas Headman is Donald Hirsch, known in hippie circles as the Chief. Make me feel sorry for you, Marian. It may help."

Quist watched the agony of decision she was involved with. She had to deny now and forever that she had any idea that Douglas Headman was her little cousin, Donald Hirsch. It might hold up. She hadn't seen Donald Hirsch

165

since he was three years old. She might get away with a denial. He could see the temptation in her eyes. With the truth she might somehow save herself. Which way to go? Which way to turn?

"Did it begin with his trying to blackmail you, Marian?" he asked.

That broke it. She moved around her chair and sat down again. She nodded slowly. "In the year before Delbert died," she said. "He turned up here one day when Delbert had gone to work; long hair, beard, dirty blue jeans and an outrageous sports shirt. The maid wanted to throw him out, but he kept insisting he was a relative of mine. When she brought up his name I felt sick at my stomach, but I agreed to see him—right here in this room. God, I didn't want him to sit down on the furniture he was so dirty—and somehow, so evil.

" 'Never expected to see me again, did you, Marian dear?'

"I told him I hadn't expected to, didn't want to now. He came very quickly to the point. He had come across a girl named Louise Hauptmann in Hollywood. He had done a little checking. She, Louise, was clearly my illegitimate child. She was, he told me, a tramp, sleeping with everyone in Hollywood.

" 'I have the feeling, dear Marian, that your elegant husband would be disturbed by the news—if it got out. And it will get out, unless—'

"Delbert was very straight-laced. Scandal was something he abhorred. And so I did the only thing I could do, Julian. I had a reasonably generous allowance. I paid him five hundred dollars a month for almost a year. Sent the money to a post office box in Hollywood. He had taken the name of David Harris. Then—then Delbert died, and Don came East again, this time for the big kill. I was very rich now, he thought. Only I wasn't."

"I know about that," Quist said.

"I ought to hate you, Julian, but somehow it's a relief to talk. Delbert's affairs were in bad shape, and the money I had was watched over by a conscientious lawyer. I couldn't pay for anything without explanations. Donald saw that I was in a corner, and he agreed to wait until things loosened up." She drew a deep breath. "The next time I saw him I didn't know him. He was Douglas Headman, sleek, well dressed, gay, charming. Maybe a week went by until we were alone one day, and with gales of laughter, he identified himself. He told me this, Julian, in my bed—which is how far I had been from recognizing Douglas Headman as that miserable, bloodsucking creep, my cousin, the Chief. It—it was his form of humor to have done what he did to me. I could have killed him but I didn't have the courage. But I was able to do the next best thing. He was in such a state of euphoria, so delighted with himself, so full of self-admiration, that he told me he no longer needed money from me. He'd found another source. He told me about Louise—Beverly. He had Johnny Sands in a trap, and he would live off Johnny forever." She drew a long, shuddering breath. "So I put the screws to him, Julian. I—I needed money desperately myself. He would share his take from Johnny with me or I would identify him to the police, who wanted him in the case of the girl who burned herself to death in Hollywood. And so—he and I lived off Johnny for the next two years."

"Until Johnny retired and stopped paying," Quist said.

"We could survive for a while," Marian said. "Then Johnny played into our hands. This benefit for Respiratory Diseases. Doug began threatening again. I—well, when Johnny came East to talk to me about it I—I tried for something else."

"Permanence," Quist said.

"He told you?"

"The kiss-and-tell kid," Quist said, "but with very high marks for your charm and talents. So, when that didn't work and Johnny ignored the threats from Headman, you turned to violence."

"No!"

"Four men are dead."

Hysteria crept into her voice. "I swear to you, Julian, Doug and I had nothing to do with that. The alibis for Doug's time are real. He hasn't been in California for more than a year. He wasn't in Chicago on Saturday. He was with me here at the time Liebman was run down on the street—with me and other people who have confirmed it for Lieutenant Kreevich. We had nothing to do with the killings, Julian, and we have no idea who is responsible. I swear that."

He sat silent, his cold eyes fixed on her.

"Oh, Doug was delighted. 'Someone is helping us no end,' he said. 'Scaring Johnny out of his wits. But we must collect from Johnny before it's too late.' I—I was sick with horror, Julian."

"The thing at Madison Square Garden was deliberately set up to clear Headman and leave him free to act?"

"Yes. How on earth did you guess that, Julian?"

"Someone gave me a lecture on top hats," Quist said. He stood up. "I'm afraid you're going to have to come with me, Marian, and and tell your story to Kreevich and the District Attorney. If you're prepared to testify against Headman things may go a little easier for you."

"There—there's no other way?"

"I'm afraid not."

She was ghost white. "Will you excuse me while I change into some sort of street clothes?"

"Of course."

She started for the door, but he stopped her. "Sheer cu-

riosity, Marian, but how did Beverly Trent—Louise—
happen to have your photograph?"

"Doug's idea of humor," she said. "On that first visit—
when he was the Chief—he stole it from here and took it
back to her. She was sharing in what they were taking
from me, I'm sure."

Quist waited. Perhaps five minutes passed when suddenly he heard someone screaming from the floor below.
He went quickly out into the hall and peered down the
stairwell. He saw the maid, down on the street-level floor,
hands covering her face, yelling her lungs out. There
were other voices, high-pitched, hysterical.

Quist didn't bother with the elevator. He ran down the
stairs to the foyer. The front door was open. The maid
just stood in the center of the room, screaming, screaming.

Quist grabbed her, shook her. "What's wrong?"

"Madam!" the maid cried. "She's out there—she must
have fallen—oh, Mother of God!"

Marian Scheer was not going to provide alibis or give
evidence against herself or anyone else.

Chapter 4

Dan garvey, fuming, sat in his personally owned little Renault car down the block from The Four Seasons Restaurant. Headman was not rushing things. There really was no reason to watch Headman tonight, he told himself. He wasn't going to be trying to collect from Johnny Sands tonight, not with Gloria to work toward. But Quist had made a point of it, and Garvey was concerned about Gloria. At least he would be at hand if she suddenly needed or wanted help.

The couple stayed for almost two hours in The Four Seasons, and Garvey fretted because he hadn't brought an extra pack of cigarettes. He kept hoping some kid would come along the street whom he could bribe to get him an extra supply.

At last Gloria and Headman emerged from the restaurant, arm in arm, laughing, very gay. Garvey swore under his breath. They had no right to be having a good time while he sat there, short of cigarettes.

The doorman hailed a taxi for them, and Garvey started the Renault's motor. He had the address of Headman's sublet from Kreevich and he expected the taxi to go uptown and east. To his surprise the cab went west, to Columbus Circle, along Central Park West, and then west again to stop in front of an undistinguished-looking brownstone. Gloria and Headman got out, still full of high spirits. The cab was paid off and disappeared toward Broadway. Gloria and Headman walked up the steps to the front door of the brownstone and Headman let them in with a key. The sonofabitch has two homes, Garvey told himself. He parked and waited, grim.

It only seemed long, less than an hour by Garvey's watch, when the front door of the brownstone opened and Headman came out. Just Headman, not Gloria. Headman started to walk briskly toward Broadway.

Garvey hesitated. His job was to keep Headman under surveillance, but he hated to drive away and leave Gloria unwatched in the brownstone. But a job is a job is a job. Perhaps Headman was just going to find a late liquor store, or a delicatessen for some sandwiches, though God knows why they should be hungry after a dinner at The Four Seasons. Perhaps Headman, the creep, was thinking ahead to breakfast. That crazy Gloria was out of her mind!

Reluctantly Garvey put the Renault in gear and trailed slowly after Headman.

At a little after eleven o'clock Quist let himself into his Beekman Place apartment. Lydia and Johnny Sands were in the living room. One look at Quist and Lydia knew that something was badly wrong. He looked tired, the spring gone out of his step. He went straight to the bar and poured himself a Jack Daniels on the rocks.

"What is it, Julian?"

He turned. His mouth was a harsh, tight line. "Marian Scheer has committed suicide," he said, "and I have to think I drove her to it."

"Julian!"

"I had it figured out down to the last dotting of an I," Quist said. "I simply didn't expect her to cop out at the

171

end." He looked at Johnny, who seemed frozen where he sat. "No question that Headman is your blackmailer, Johnny. And Headman is Hirsch and also the Chief. It's a long story, but Marian was involved in it in a sort of oblique fashion. She was blackmailing Headman and collecting part of what you paid him."

"So his alibis won't stand up," Johnny said. "He killed Eddie and the others. So help me God, when I get my hands on him I'll—"

"Without Marian to testify we need to go ahead," Quist said. "We need to catch him with his hands on the money."

The telephone rang.

"That may be Daniel reporting in," Quist said.

Lydia picked up the phone and said, "Hello." She turned slowly to Quist, her eyes very wide. "It's for you, Julian," she said. "It's Douglas Headman!"

Quist took the phone from her. His voice sounded flat. "Yes, Headman?"

"What a terribly clever fellow you are, Quist," Headman said. There was laughter behind it. "Oh, I know your phone is bugged, dad. I'll give the number to the cops if it will make things easier for you."

"What's on your mind?" Quist asked.

"Money, of course," Headman said. "Have you been listening to your radio? If you have, you know that I know that our maid Marian took a swan dive off the roof of her house. Did you drive her to it, Quist?"

"What do you want?" Quist said. His voice was unsteady with suppressed anger.

"Like I said, Dad, money. This time you will deliver it, Quist, and without any tricks. I don't trust Johnny not to blow his stack. You, I know, will play it cool because of your lovely Miss Chard. She really is a doll, Quist."

"What about Gloria?"

"You will play it cool, dad, or you will have to find a new receptionist. Dear little Gloria will no longer be pretty enough to sit at your circular desk and charm the customers. She will look as though somebody had tried to make a rare hamburger out of her face. I kid you not, dad, and I say it just once. She will wish she was dead, which is a pity because she's so full of life. Now listen."

Quist's lips moved stiffly. "I'm listening."

"You will bring the suitcase, with the money in it, to the northeast corner of Broadway and Fifty-seventh Street. There is a wire trash basket there. You will put the suitcase in it, and you will then go the hell away from there. Clear?"

"So far."

"You will bring the bag at precisely one o'clock," Headman said. He giggled. "That will give you almost two hours to think of all the ways you might doublecross me. But while you're thinking, dad, keep remembering glorious Gloria and how unglorious your treachery will make her. All clear?"

"Clear."

"I wish I could wait until after banking hours tomorrow, I'd double the amount of money. But I have a feeling our Marian may have talked too much. Isn't it strange how noble people can become all of a sudden? However, I suspect you've always been noble, dad. Stay that way, if you care about Gloria Chard. Be prompt."

The phone clicked off.

Quist replaced the receiver with a hand that wasn't steady. In a colorless voice he laid it out for Lydia and Johnny. While he was still telling them the phone rang again. It was Kreevich's man who was monitoring the calls in the basement.

"We were able to trace the call, Mr. Quist. It was a coin box in a street booth near Lincoln Center on the

West Side. We'll have a patrol car see if they can spot Headman."

"No!" Quist said sharply. "Let him alone. Can you reach the Lieutenant?"

"I think so."

"Get him to call me as quickly as you can. Did you listen in on the call? If not, listen to the tape and you'll understand why I don't want Headman interferred with."

Lydia was standing close to Quist, her hand on his arm. "Do you really think he'd hurt Gloria?"

"He's crazy," Johnny said. "He'd do anything to anyone."

"He was somewhere, laughing, when a girl burned herself to death at his suggestion," Quist said. "Dan is what worries me. He's watching him. If Headman spots him—"

"Call him off!" Johnny said.

"Where is he?" Quist said.

"You know where this apartment is he sublets?" Johnny asked. "Where else would he take Gloria but his apartment?"

"I could go there," Lydia said, "spot Dan, and call him off."

"If Kreevich calls, he can get a squad car there quicker than one of us could make it," Quist said. He struck his forehead with the palm of his hand. "I let her go with him. I should have known he wouldn't have had his eye on anything but the main chance. I let Marian get away from me when I'd driven her right up against the wall. God!"

The phone rang again and it was Kreevich.

"You have the address of Headman's sublet apartment?" Quist asked him.

"Sure I do."

"I've been being very smart, very clever," Quist said. "I

thought we could trap Headman for you." He explained what Garvey was doing, and then detailed the phone call from Headman. "I can't call Dan off because I don't know where he is. But he may be outside Headman's apartment, waiting in a small Renault sedan. You agree he must be called off, don't you?"

"I wish to God you didn't think of yourself as a genius," Kreevich said.

"I, too."

"Why do you suppose he's given us two hours to stew in?" the Lieutenant asked. "Hold it a minute, I'll have a patrol car look for Garvey."

Quist waited, the lines at the corners of his eyes etched deep by anxiety.

Kreevich came back. "Car on the way," he said. "They should be there in two or three minutes, have Garvey away in five—if they find him. You got an answer to my question? Why two hours?"

"A getaway is my guess," Quist said. "A plane reservation for somewhere—Mexico, the Islands. He's given himself just time to grab the money and make connections with the plane—before we can start any kind of search."

"Will he have your girl with him, do you think?"

"Who knows?"

"If my boys find Garvey he'll know where she is. If it's the apartment, should we risk breaking in?"

"He could be standing over her with a knife—acid—God knows what," Quist said. "If we trap him he won't give up. He'll hurt Gloria to punish us."

"So we let him slip away," Kreevich said.

"And pray," Quist said.

He left the phone and began to move around the room, his fists clenched in the pockets of his blue jacket. Lydia went to him.

"You mustn't blame yourself, darling," she said. "Gloria knew she was running risks; she knew he might be a killer."

"But I didn't," he said. "I knew he might be a killer but I was naïve enough to think he was really attracted by Gloria. A kid playing with matches is what I was."

"So you deliver the money and then we find her," Lydia said.

"You have ideas where we start to look?" he asked. "Of course, as Kreevich suggested, he may take her with him. Then what?"

Kreevich was back on the phone, sounding grim. "No sign of your friend Garvey in the neighborhood of the sublet," he told Quist. "You'll take the money?"

"Yes."

"We'll circle the area."

"But even if you bump into him, let him go till we've found Gloria," Quist said.

At twelve-thirty Quist left his apartment, carrying a hundred thousand dollars in the pigskin bag. He picked up a taxi on Second Avenue and instructed the driver to take him to Fifty-fifth Street and Broadway.

It was a beautifully clear night after the storm. A full moon bathed the city with its pale light. There was very little traffic and Quist reached his destination well ahead of time. He stood in the shadow of a building, his eyes on his watch. He allowed himself exactly three minutes to reach the trash basket on the corner of Fifty-seventh Street. He could feel little trickles of sweat running down inside his shirt. He was dealing with a madman. He had to be exact about following instructions.

At three minutes to one he started to walk briskly toward the trash basket two blocks away. A man passed him, headed downtown. Across the street a couple looked through the window of an automobile showroom. A taxi with an off-duty sign showing swept past him, headed in the same direction. No police. No one who might be remotely connected with Kreevich.

He reached the trash basket with fifteen seconds to spare. His watch raised, he waited until the precise moment and then dropped the bag into the wire receptacle.

Perhaps the hardest thing he could ever remember doing was to turn his back and walk away.

Dan Garvey told himself that Headman was some kind of monumental screwball. He wines and dines a girl at the most elegant and expensive restaurant in town, takes her to a little West Side hideout, leaves here there, supposedly to run an errand that will add to the pleasure of the evening—and doesn't go back!

Following Headman as he walked toward Broadway from the brownstone where he'd left Gloria, Garvey saw his man stop at one of the pay-phone booths located on a street corner. Even at a distance Garvey could see that Headman was enjoying his conversation with someone; much laughter and evident pleasure. The conversation ended, Headman came out of the booth, looked up and down the street, and then headed across Broadway toward a rather crummy-looking bar. Garvey pulled the Renault to the curb, halfway down the block, and waited. Headman, he told himself, would reappear presently, carrying a supply of liquor. He undoubtedly had an in with the management of this place which made it simpler than hunting down some liquor store that might still be open. As a matter of fact, at eleven-thirty at night there probably weren't any open liquor stores.

But Headman didn't come out. Ten, twenty minutes went by. Garvey swore softly to himself. Maybe there was a back entrance to this place. If Headman had used it then it seemed likely that he had spotted Garvey; the most direct way back to Gloria was the way he had come. At the end of a half an hour Garvey got out of his car and walked along in the shadow of the buildings to the front of the bar—O'Connell's Bar and Grill. He walked by the door, his hat pulled down, and got a glimpse of the interior. Headman was there, sitting at a table at the rear of the place, alone. He had a tall glass in front of him that might be a gin and tonic, might be just plain soda water. He was smoking a cigarette, looking very relaxed. As Garvey passed, Headman was studying his wrist watch.

This was the ever-living end. The man sat there, drinking, while Gloria, presumably panting with impatience, waited for him half a block away. This must be some kind of erotic nonsense.

Garvey went back to the Renault and waited. Another half hour went by and then Headman came out onto the street. No package, no liquor supply. He stood at the curb until a cruising taxi came his way. Garvey started his motor. Headman wouldn't take a cab to go a block and a half, or would he? Everything about him was crazy. The taxi headed downtown, away from the brownstone where Gloria was waiting. It turned east on Fifty-fourth Street, crossed over Broadway and headed north, and stopped at the curb. Headman remained inside.

Then Garvey felt himself jolted as though he'd touched a live electric wire. Across the street he saw Quist, carrying the familiar pigskin bag, walking briskly uptown. The game was apparently on.

Headman's taxi didn't move. Quist had reached the corner of Fifty-seventh Street. He paused by a wire trash basket, looked at his watch, and then dropped the suitcase into the wire basket. He turned and walked away.

Still Headman's taxi didn't move. It didn't move until Quist had reached a corner a block away and turned east, out of sight. Then the taxi started. The Renault moved at the same time.

Just short of the trash basket where the pigskin bag rested the taxi stopped again. The rear door opened and Headman got out. He moved toward the basket and the bag.

In his salad days in professional football Garvey had played at free safety. They used to mention him in the same category as the New York Giants' Spider Lockhart in what is called the "safety blitz." At the snap of the ball the free safety charges through to the other team's quarterback who is fading to pass. As Headman reached the trash basket Garvey was under a full head of steam. Just as Headman reached out for the pigskin bag he was hit by a flying head-and-shoulder block that sent him flying through the air a good ten yards from the bag which he had never reached. Garvey was on top of him; Garvey had him by the head, which he banged against the pavement.

Headman lay very still, a little gush of blood running out of the corner of his mouth. There was a squeal of tires on pavement. The taxi driver was taking off in a hurry. He wanted no part of what was going on.

Garvey stood up, bruised and angry. The town seemed to be deserted. He went over the trash basket and picked out the bag with the money in it. Then he bent down over Headman, took him by the back of his coat collar, and dragged him, like a sack of potatoes, toward the Renault. He managed to pile the unconscious man and the bag into the car, got in himself, and headed uptown toward the brownstone where Gloria was presumably waiting.

Garvey's anger was somehow centered on Gloria. Going out with a miserable creep like Headman, a murderer, a blackmailer. Well, he'd present her with her

179

lover boy!

Outside the Brownstone Headman hadn't stirred. Garvey, coldly clinical, checked to make sure he was alive. He was. He pulled the unconscious body out of the car. With the suitcase under one arm, he dragged Headman across the sidewalk and into the vestibule of the building. He glanced at the names in the little brass plates. "David Harris, 1-C." Headman was still using old names, the jerk.

Garvey tried the bell for 1-C and got no answer. Gloria apparently wasn't answering the doorbell. Garvey rang four other bells. The door began to click and he opened it, dragging Headman behind him. Someone called down from upstairs. "Who is it?"

Garvey marched toward the rear. 1-C would be at the back. A woman screamed. "I'm calling the police," she shouted at Garvey.

"You just do that," Garvey said.

He got to the door of 1-C and banged on it. The little idiot wasn't even going to answer that. He backed away and charged it. The door splintered and Garvey kicked it open. Then he dragged Headman into the room—and he saw Gloria.

She was sitting in a chair, facing him, her hands and feet tied, a piece of adhesive tape over her mouth. Garvey looked down at Headman—and kicked him.

Then he went to Gloria. "Love's young dream," he said. "This is going to hurt." He zipped the piece of tape off her mouth.

"Oh God, Daniel, am I glad to see you!" she said.

"I've always told you I should be the man in your life," Garvey said. He bent down and undid he pieces of clothesline that had chafed her wrists and ankles.

"Is he—is he dead?" she asked, her wide eyes fixed on Headman.

"Not yet," Garvey said. He walked across the room to a telephone and dialed Quist's number.

"Julian? I got him—and the money," he said.

Quist's voice was tense. "Gloria's in danger somewhere, Daniel. Can you get him to talk?"

"Gloria's here, chum, ruffled but all right."

"Where are you?"

"West Sixty-fifth Street," Garvey said. He gave Quist the address.

"Kreevich is cruising that part of town," Quist said. "I'll have him there on the double."

"Good." Garvey glanced at Gloria. "When our Gloria has told Kreevich her story she's going to need a little soothing. See you around."

Quist put down the phone. Lydia and Johnny Sands were waiting for him to tell them what had happened.

"It's all over," Quist said. "Daniel got him—and the bag. Gloria's safe. I didn't get the details from him, but they can wait."

"Thank God!" Lydia said.

"All over," Johnny said. "Boy, I think I can sleep for a week now. I don't know if you can guess what it's been like, pals, waiting for the axe to fall."

"I can guess," Quist said. He went over to Lydia and put his hands on her shoulders. "Run along home, love," he said. "It's been a long day."

"Julian!" She looked hurt.

"You don't have to play it cool for me, pals," Johnny said. "Once I've had a nightcap and hit the sack I won't know you're alive for the next twenty-four hours."

"Go home, doll," Quist said.

"Whatever you say," Lydia said. She sounded brittle. "It's been nice knowing you all."

Quist bent down and kissed her cheek. "Don't be childish," he said. He went to the door with her.

Johnny was at the bar. "Join me in a nightcap?" he asked.

"Why not?" Quist looked worn, tired.

"It'll be interesting to know how Headman faked those alibis," Johnny said, "but I can wait. I can wait forever now that it's over."

Quist took a Jack Daniels from Johnny and wandered over to the terrace door with it. "It's not over, Johnny," he said.

"As far as I'm concerned," Johnny said. "Let Kreevich sweat over the details. I can be a free man again, thank God."

Quist turned and faced him. There was pain in his pale blue eyes. "Not free, Johnny. Not ever free again," he said.

"I can stand the notoriety," Johnny said. "My friends will forget it after a while. My public will forget it."

"I wish they could, Johnny. Wish it with all my heart," Quist said. "I'm shaken down to my very roots by the horror of it, but I still feel a kind of sympathy for you."

The smile froze on Johnny's face. "What in hell are you talking about, pal?"

"I'd like to say it quickly and be done with it, Johnny," Quist said. "Headman's alibis will stand up. You know it as well as I do, because Headman didn't kill anybody—at least none of the four people we're concerned with."

"Then who in God's name did?"

"You, Johnny," Quist said very quietly.

A nerve twitched high up on Johnny's cheek. "Don't tell me you're starting to buy the frame-up, pal. Headman framed me."

"No, Johnny. You made it look like a frame-up, because by drawing attention to yourself you actually looked innocent. Mr. Chambrun's top hat theory all over again."

182

"Oh, come off it, Julian." Johnny reached for the bottle of Irish. "I'm not in the mood for fun and games. This is a joke, isn't it?"

"We know most of the story now," Quist said. "Headman—known as the Chief then—was at your party. He found Beverly Trent dead in your bedroom, read the note. He hung around and saw what you and Sabol and Liebman did about it. He saw his way to a get-rich-quick scheme. That's all he knew, Johnny, but it was enough to make you pay. But that's all there ever was or has been to Headman's part in this. He and Marian bled you. That's it, the total Headman story."

"So I stopped paying and he then started killing off everyone involved to scare me into resuming," Johnny said. His face was a sickly gray color.

"No, Johnny. The first thing that bothered me was the death of Marshall, the Hollywood cop. Marshall wasn't part of that party night. How could Headman know about him? No way, unless you or Marshall told him. I began to question Headman's guilt then. The candlestick convinced me."

"What are you talking about?"

"How was it, Johnny? You paid and paid and then you quit. You quit paying, and you quit your career. That career was all that mattered to you in the world. Every day without it was torture. Then came the chance to do the benefit at the Garden. You could start all over again. When it was announced that you'd do it, the blackmailer—oh, it was Headman—threatened again. That, my poor friend, is when you went off your rocker. You reasoned it out. Headman never entered your mind as a possibility. It had to be one of the four people who knew the truth about Beverly Trent—Marshall, the cop, Sabol, Liebman, or poor little Eddie Wismer. One of your friends was a Judas. And so you weren't having any more, and you decided to wipe out all four of them."

Johnny swallowed a glass of Irish and repoured. The neck of the bottle rattled against the rim of his glass.

"The first three were easy, and cleverly planned. You couldn't bring yourself to believe it could be Eddie. But after the other three were dead you got a call from the blackmailer. So—God help him—it had to be Eddie."

A curious choking sound came from Johnny.

"I hadn't quite figured it then," Quist said, "and I—I pushed Eddie over the cliff by urging him to go away. You couldn't let him go. He could blackmail you from a distance then. And so—you killed him with that candlestick, walked calmly out of that death room and to Marian's party. I wondered at the time why the murderer had come unprepared, used something that just happened to come to hand. Then I realized how it had to be. Nobody came. You were already there. You had plenty of time to decide what to use. You had to do it then or Eddie would be gone. Did he plead with you, Johnny? Did he tell you how much he loved you? Did he protest, while you were killing him, that he would never in God's world have betrayed you?"

"Poor little bastard," Johnny said in a cracked voice. "I thought it had to be him. *It had to!*"

Quist leaned on the back of a chair. His legs felt rubbery under him. A good man had been tortured into madness. Headman, without blood on his hands, was responsible for five deaths; five, because Johnny was as good as dead.

And then Quist found himself staring into the barrel of a gun.

"It's your peashooter, pal," Johnny said, "so you know it works."

Quist didn't move. His hands were gripping the back of the chair. "Has it gotten that easy for you, Johnny? Have

184

you gotten to like it? Killing?"

"You don't give me much time to figure things, pal," Johnny said. His face was glistening with sweat. "I don't intend to turn myself over to the cops. I don't intend to face a trial. I've got to get out of here, pal, and figure things. If you try to stop me I don't have any choice."

"There's no escape, Johnny," Quist said.

"Don't force my hand, Julian," Johnny said.

"Drop it, Sands," a harsh voice said from behind Quist.

Johnny turned, his trigger finger squeezing at the gun. Quist hurled the chair at him and dove. The gun seemed to explode in his face, and there was a second shot from somewhere else.

Quist scrambled up to his feet. One of Kreevich's men was grappling with Johnny. A second was coming down the stairs from the floor above, followed by Lydia.

"I changed your mind—about going home," she said. She tried to laugh, and instead there were tears, and she was in Quist's arms, clinging to him. "The way you told me to go—I knew something was up."

"Idiot," he said. His lips touched her hair.

"I eavesdropped," she said.

"Bad manners," he said, and kissed her cheek.

"When you started to unwind it I—I went for Kreevich's men. I gave one of them my front door key and let the other one in the back way." Her arms tightened around him. "Poor Johnny," she said.

Without looking back, Johnny Sands was on his way out, handcuffs on his wrists. There would be no more golden trumpet, no more joyful songs.